Early Snow

Kevin Wolf

Other books by Kevin Wolf

The Homeplace
Brokeheart
A Town Called Vengance
The Bootheel
Trailridge

Chapter 1

October 30, 1982

By noon, the autumn sky had turned from blue to the color of road asphalt. Treetops bent in the wind funneling into the canyon from the high peaks. Stray snowflakes splattered the windshield, turned into tiny droplets, and in an instant were gone.

My best friend and new boss, Dalton Cummings, pulled his pickup into a parking spot at the back of the big, white hotel and killed the engine. "The truck with the paintings is supposed to be here in about an hour." He pulled up the sleeve of his flannel shirt and checked his Timex for the tenth time. "We'll leave our gear in the pickup. I'll let the hotel manager know we're here. You see if you can find,"—He snatched a clipboard from the dashboard and flipped through the pages. "Damn it, I can never remember her..."

"Porsche Hurt," I told him. "Porsche. Like the car. Hurt, like ouch."

"That's one of those damn made-up New York City names if I've ever heard one. Her folks never gave it to her."

"You've said that before." Then it hit me. I held back a smile. "I know what's going on. Ex-game warden Dalton Cummings is nervous about his first paying job since retirement. What could it be?" I enjoyed the edge I had over my friend.

Cummings turned toward the window. His breath painted a gray haze on the glass.

"Let me guess." I wanted to see his face, but he wouldn't turn back. "The man who fought forest fires, rescued lost campers, and saved fish and wildlife for generations to come is afraid of a New York woman."

"That ain't it."

"Then what?"

He shook his head, and the brim of his Stetson left a mark on the fogged window. "I don't like hotels," he mumbled.

"What?"

"Hotels." He clamped both hands on the steering wheel. "I'd rather be in my own bed." He stared straight ahead. "I do fine in a sleepin' bag in the backcountry. But there's somethin' about a little old mint on a fluffy pillow and turned-down sheets that makes me all crawly." He shook like he was cold. "It's all too fancy."

"Don't worry." I bit back a laugh. "It's just two nights. You probably won't get any sleep anyway." I couldn't resist adding one more thing. "The ghosts will keep you awake."

Cummings jerked up on the door handle and glanced sideways at me. He raised his middle finger. "Screw you, Hogan."

—

A handful of dried leaves skittered from the front doors onto the lobby's hardwood. Smoke from the fire that crackled in the fireplace blended with the scent of bacon and warm maple syrup on the guests' plates as they enjoyed a late breakfast in the restaurant. A white-haired couple sat on a Queen Anne loveseat and watched the first snowflakes through the lobby's picture windows. Her head rested on his shoulder.

Except for the white Reeboks on the old man's feet, it could have been a scene from the first dozen years after the old hotel opened. My wife told me that she would have enjoyed that more genteel time. When women chose their best dresses and dined on china, with crystal and silver. When blue jeans were reserved for the afternoon trail rides, and tennis shoes were worn only for tennis. During our vacation nights in the old hotel, we made plans to move to Estes Park. I had even told Jenny that one day I could see myself working at the old hotel—perhaps leading the historic tours or suggesting places to fish for the guests. But things had changed. Jenny was gone. But a small part of those dreams had come true. I'd be working at the hotel for the next two days.

A man in a dark blue blazer with brass buttons kneeled by the fireplace hearth. He split a piece of firewood with a hatchet and tossed the pine logs into the fireplace. He tucked the hatchet between the stone fireplace and the woodbox and turned his back to the fire.

I tugged at the zipper of my down jacket and crossed the lobby to where he stood. "I'm with Cummings Security. Here to help with the art show. I'm Guy Hogan."

"Jim Hayes, Mr. Hogan." He pushed a shock of faded blond hair off his forehead. "They told me to expect you." His eyes narrowed as if trying to memorize my face. "Am I right? You were the one who helped solve that elk poaching scandal up in the park. About the time of the Lawn Lake flood, wasn't it? A woman was killed. Do I remember correctly?"

I bit down on my lip and nodded, then held out my hand

Hayes's grip was soft, and his face was tired from too many years of being too polite to too many people, but he held a friendly smile.

"My boss is letting your manager know we're here," I told

him. "I'm supposed to find Porsche Hurt and see what she needs for us to do 'til the truck arrives."

A round woman in a shiny purple jogging suit pushed in between us. "Excuse me." She looked up at Hayes. "I'm supposed to be on the hotel tour. You know the one that shows us all the haunted places and tells us about the ghosts." She panted. "I lost track of the time—too many prunes at breakfast—have they left yet? The tour, I mean."

Hayes's attention went from me to the woman. "Mrs. Randolph, isn't it?"

"*Mizzz* Randolph." She took off her eyeglasses and left them hanging from a beaded chain around her neck. She batted her eyes at the concierge and patted the gooey nest of gray spikes that was her hair.

"Yes, *Ms.* Randolph. The tour just left. You can catch them downstairs."

"Have I missed anything?"

"No. But you'll need to hurry."

She fumbled with her glasses. "Was that Odyssey Pruitt I saw outside? You know, the artist. She was all bundled up, but I'm sure it was her."

Hayes focused on the woman as if she were the only other person in the room. "It very well could have been. I saw her in the lobby earlier this morning. She was an employee here at the hotel several years ago, so she's familiar with the area."

"I know all that." Ms. Randolph lowered her voice. "I'm one of her biggest fans. I already own two of her paintings. I intend to buy another one at her show." With that, she waddled across the lobby and down the stairs.

The concierge smiled at me and shook his head.

"Odyssey?" I asked. "That's whose paintings I'm here to guard?"

"Yeah. It was Audrey when she worked here. Strange girl. A mousy little thing who kept to herself. She"—Hayes's fingers made quote marks in the air—"found herself. Started painting.

And changed her name somewhere along the line. They pay me to know such things." He peeked over his shoulder at the registration counter. "Though this weekend I was asked not to tell that bit of the story."

The front doors opened. Two women in ski jackets and scarves stood in the opening. A bellman with an overloaded luggage cart stopped short of running the two over.

Hayes nodded at the door. "Looks like I'm needed."

"Porsche Hurt?"

"Follow *Mizz* Randolph. Ms. Hurt's with the ghost tour."

"How will I know which one is her?"

"Oh, you'll know her. She'll be the only woman less than sixty in that group." His eyebrows arched. "And Mr. Hogan, she's something to see."

—

Three more women as round and colorful as Ms. Randolph squeezed into the narrow corridor at the bottom of the stairway. The floor cocked slightly off level, and someone had removed the light bulbs from every other fixture down the hall. Even at nearly noon, the corridor seemed as shadowy as twilight.

The ladies jostled closer to a tall man in the same blue blazer as Hayes's. His hair was as gray as everyone around him. Somewhere in the middle of the group, an arm raised, and the blaze from a flashbulb filled the hall.

The tour leader blinked but never lost the rhythm of his well-practiced spiel. "This location was selected for this hotel not only for the view of the valley but also because the natural limestone and quartz formations could be used as the foundation for this glorious building. It is well known that quartz is a conductor of psychic energy. That would be one of the factors that make his hotel very special."

Ms. Randolph nodded, and a smile beamed on her face.

The leader gestured to a padlocked door marked *employees only*.

Ms. Randolph pushed past the other ladies for a better look. Her bright nylon jogging suit swished as one of her thick thighs rubbed the other.

The tour leader continued, "In the early days, this hotel was quite isolated, and the staff was housed in buildings behind the main structure."

Ms. Randolph stood on her tiptoes and waved her hand to interrupt the man. "Is that where Odyssey Pruitt lived when she worked here?"

"Why, yes."

"Will we—"

"We will discuss that when we view the employee dormitories." He cleared his throat and glanced at the other ladies. "As I said, tunnels were built to connect the hotel with the staff housing. During construction, there was a cave-in, and one of the workers was killed." It went very quiet. Even Ms. Randolph's nylon ceased its rustle. "Today, our marketing and purchasing departments have their offices on this level. Just a few weeks ago, one of the staff, who had stayed to work late, swore they heard the sound of a hammer striking stone." He paused. A practiced pause, I guessed. "Could it be that the trapped soul of that worker is still seeking to escape from his cold tomb?"

Ms. Randolph's hand covered her mouth, but a tiny gasp escaped.

"If you'll count with me, this is the first of the seven ghosts we'll discuss on our tour."

I wasn't counting. I needed to find Porsche Hurt. If what Hayes had said about being young and attractive was true, she wasn't part of this group. I glanced at my watch. The truck with the paintings was due any minute. Cummings would be looking for me. Given his mood from earlier, I needed to find Miss Hurt soon.

Another round of flashbulbs popped. The tour followed their leader toward a shaft of daylight shining through the window of a ground-level door at the far end of the hallway.

From an alcove, a woman I hadn't noticed before stepped out. She could have been one of the hotel visitors from those gentler times. A pale gray skirt fell to just below her knees. Ruffles on the front of her blouse rippled when she moved. Perhaps this was ghost number two. But her high heels tapped over the rough concrete floor. She paused; her face hidden in the glare of one of the lights. Her hair was blonde, and the lights made it golden.

There is a socially accepted length of time a man can look at a beautiful woman before that stare becomes a gawk. I was dangerously close to breaking that rule.

I swallowed and mustered the strength to call out. "Miss Hurt?"

The woman turned; her face still lost in the harsh shine.

Before she could speak, the door at the end of the hallway burst wide open. Like the whistle of a runaway locomotive hurtling through a tunnel, a woman's shriek filled the hallway.

"Odyssey?" Ms. Randolph shuffled toward the figure who had screamed. "Dear, what's wrong?"

I was moving toward the open door before I realized it. In the narrow hallway, I shoved past the woman in gray, around the ladies on the tour, and by their leader. Ms. Randolph's arms wrapped around the small woman who'd come from the outside. "Odyssey. Child, what is it?" she asked.

Snowflakes matted in Odyssey's hair. She buried her face in her hands.

"Odyssey?" Ms. Randolph squeezed her tighter.

The girl pulled her hands away from her face. "Someone," she gasped. "Someone cut off his head."

—

Someone cut off his head.

Snow swirled off the building. It hung in fresh, new clumps on the pine tree branches and covered the lawn near the hotel.

I could make out Odyssey's footprints, but fluffy flakes as big as quarters quickly covered the marks.

Someone cut off his—

She'd seen a body.

I grabbed the frame around the open door and looked at the young woman in Ms. Randolph's arms. "Odyssey, where is it?"

She raised her face from the woman's shoulder. Melted snow and tears blended with streaks of dark makeup on her cheeks. Her eyes stared at me, but seemed to see nothing.

I made my voice softer. "Where is it, Odyssey?"

Her lips trembled. "The tree. The big tree."

Between the building and the gazebo where tourists gathered on summer nights stood a pine tree taller than the fourth-story windows of the hotel. I squinted into the flurry of falling flakes, pushed off the doorframe, and started for the tree.

Someone—

That someone could still be out there.

It was two dozen slick steps to the pine tree. Its branches had been trimmed away as high as a man could reach, and a wooden bench for tired visitors rested against the trunk. Stalks of autumn-dried wildflowers dusted with white crowded near its base.

A severed head. There would be blood. Lots of blood.

But no red stained the white. No headless body waited in the falling snow.

I sucked in what might have been my first breath since Odyssey screamed. With the toe of my boot, I swept away the snow near the old bench. Nothing.

Voices and the rustling sound of nylon on nylon moved behind me. I whipped around. The ladies from the tour huddled together, watching what I would do next. Odyssey was still in Ms. Randolph's arms.

"Where did you see it, Odyssey?" I spoke softly.

She raised her arm and pointed.

Just where the path turned toward the hotel, fading

footprints left their marks where someone had stopped. Just a bump in the snow.

Not a body. Bile rushed into the back of my throat. *Only the head.* Snowflakes collected on the upright hairs on the back of my neck.

"Go on back to the hotel. All of you," I said over my shoulder.

No one moved.

"Please go back inside."

They stayed rooted in the places they stood.

I dropped onto my knees with my back to the ladies, shielding them from the horror I was about to uncover.

It's small. Too small to be a person's head. What if? No, it can't be. A child's head?

My mind formed a prayer. I reached out and brushed away the thin layer of new snow. The hair was wet. And brown. I pushed more snow away. Relief let my shoulders drop.

"Ladies, it's a dead rabbit." Brown-gray fur and a white cotton-ball tail. I turned to the group. "Odyssey, did you see this rabbit?"

She pulled away from Ms. Randolph and nodded. "But someone cut off its head. The spirits did it. I know they did. It's a warning. They don't want me here."

The woman in gray stepped between the ladies and where I kneeled. "Enough excitement for now." She spread out her arms and waved her hands toward the hotel. "Go on inside before we all freeze." She placed her arm around Odyssey's shoulder and gave a squeeze. "It's just a rabbit, dear. Some old coyote was hunting for his dinner, that's all. Happens out here all the time. You remember."

Ms. Randolph tugged on Odyssey's coat sleeve, pulled her close, and wrapped her arm around the girl's waist. The two followed the others into the hotel.

I looked down at the dead rabbit. The woman in gray was right. The flower gardens and bushes around the hotel were a perfect place for rabbits to hide. Coyotes or foxes might slip in at night and pick off a cottontail for their supper. Something could have scared this one off before it could eat its kill. What she said made perfect sense.

Except that the coyote that killed this rabbit carried a knife.

The rabbit's head had been sliced neatly off, and I couldn't find the head anywhere in the nearby snow.

The woman in gray moved closer to me. "None of those ladies will sleep tonight." Droplets from the melting snow clung to the ends of her hair and collected in the folds of the lace on the front of her blouse. In the shadowy hallway, the light had made her hair shine like gold. Outside, it was the color of caramel. Faded freckles played across her high cheekbones, and her eyes were a warm brown. I had been right to stare at her in the hall.

"Yeah, I'm not so sure I will either. Sleep tonight, I mean." I was staring again. Maybe gawking. And this woman knew about coyotes. "You're not Porsche Hurt, are you?"

"No. My name is Shelby Guess. I work for the hotel's marketing department. I was just coming out of my office when—" She nodded toward the rabbit in the snow. "And you are?"

"Guy Hogan. I'm with Cummings Security. Here to help with the art show."

"That's why you asked for Porsche. I see now. I work in marketing for the hotel, and I'm the liaison for the event." She shivered at the cold. "Let's go inside, and I'll help you find Porsche."

"Let me take care of this." I pointed at the rabbit. "Give me a minute and I'll meet you inside."

She turned, and her long legs carried her easily over the snowy ground, back to the hotel.

I scooped up the rabbit. Rigor mortis stiffened the little body. It had been dead for some time. Dark blood seeped from where the head had been cut from the neck. No tear marks on the fur. No holes from a predator's teeth.

Maybe it was the spirits.

I fished a paper bag from the trash bin outside the hotel door and slipped the dead rabbit inside. I tucked the bundle under the trash can.

Maybe I'd show this to Cummings. Just to see what he thinks about a headless rabbit.

It wasn't the cold that prickled my neck when I reached for the door handle. It was that feeling that someone was watching.

Jim Hayes stood at the corner window of the floor just above me. He stepped back when I raised my face.

—

I brushed the snow off my shoulders and followed Shelby up the stairs to the lobby. The ladies on the ghost tour, Ms. Randolph included, peered out of the open brass doors of the hotel elevator, while their leader pushed his way inside. The door moved closed. Cables strained, and the arrow on the semicircle above the door slowly swung in an arc as the elevator moved from the lobby to the upper floors.

"That's Porsche there." Shelby pointed to the foot of the staircase. "With Odyssey."

I guessed Porsche was ten years younger than Shelby. Jet-black hair fell to her shoulders. She was slender. Her tight jeans were tucked into knee-high riding boots. The kind of boots that were designed for sidewalks, not horses. She wore a snug black turtleneck. What Hayes had said was right. She was "something."

Porsche put both of her hands on Odyssey's shoulders. She leaned close and kissed the artist on the forehead. Odyssey climbed the stairs and paused at the landing. Porsche smiled and waved. Then, Odyssey disappeared into the second-floor hallway.

Shelby gave a "follow me" wiggle with her finger. "Come on. I'll introduce you."

We crossed the lobby.

"Porsche, this is Guy Hogan. Mr. Hogan is with the security company, helping with Odyssey's art show. He's been looking for you."

Maybe Porsche Hurt wasn't ten years younger than Shelby. There was a lot of makeup on that face. I surveyed the front of her sweater, felt guilty, and raised my eyes.

"Uh—I, er." I couldn't make my mouth work.

Shelby hid a smile with her hand.

I tried again. "Uh. Th-they said you were with the tour. I went downstairs."

Porsche's eyes opened wide. "Are you the man who helped Odyssey?"

I nodded. It was easier than speaking.

"Oh, thank you. Creative people like Odyssey can be very high-strung. She's quite nervous, what with her show opening tomorrow and all the celebrities that have said they will be here—you know, John Denver just confirmed. Things are coming together. But it's all been very hard on her. Seeing that dead animal in the snow upset her so. Poor girl, the police in New York just arrested a man who was following her everywhere. Making the most terrible threats. She's doing much better now." Porsche leaned forward. She whispered, "Odyssey has a gift. Some might think it's a bit of a curse. She sees things."

I drew a circle on the inside of my cheek with the tip of my tongue.

Porsche smiled, with big, perfect teeth framed by equally perfect lips with perfectly applied lipstick. "She must. It's the subject of all her paintings. You know what I mean, don't you?"

"I'm sorry, ma'am, I don't."

Porsche cocked her head. "Odyssey's paintings are images of the spirits that appeared to her when she worked here. A little ghost peeking around the corner of a hallway. A phantom on the stairs. A devilish imp riding the elevator. Since they made Mr. King's book into a movie. You know, *The Shining*. Her work has become extremely popular with a certain group of collectors. What she sold for a few dollars at flea markets now brings thousands."

"Oh." I remembered Odyssey's tearful warning that those spirits might not want her here. *And how much more would those paintings go for if her fans believed that?*

Dalton came around the corner of the registration desk, nursing a mug of steaming coffee.

"Ladies, this is Dalton Cummings," I told them as he stepped up. "Boss, meet Shelby Guess. She's with the hotel."

Cummings's free hand touched the brim of his Stetson. "Pleased, ma'am. You were the one who called about us workin' for you?"

Shelby smiled. "I was."

"And boss, this is Porsche Hurt," I said. "It's her art show."

The old ranger's motion to tip his hat stalled at the same instant his gaze found Porsche's sweater.

"Yeah," was the only word that came out of his mouth. He brought the coffee to his lips and took a noisy gulp.

Porsche beamed. "Really, it's Odyssey's show. I'm only her business manager. I handle all the arrangements so she has time to be creative." She glanced at her gold wristwatch. "Has there been any word on when the truck with her paintings will arrive?"

Dalton glubbed down the next swallow of his coffee. He came up for air and spoke. "The hotel manager just got a call. Truck driver radioed his boss to tell him that he's runnin' late. It's snowin' hard in the canyon 'tween here and Loveland, and I guess a semi got all kitty-wumpus across the road and tied everything up for a good while. Our truck's rollin' now, but it could be another hour before he gets here."

Porsche's face turned to a little girl's pout. The ends of her lips turned down, and I watched a flake from her thick makeup drift to the floor.

Shelby pointed across the lobby. "While we wait, let me

show you the space we'll be using for the show. It's called the Piano Room." She started across the lobby, Porsche took her arm, and Dalton and I followed. "Remember that this hotel opened in the early nineteen-hundreds. Back then, after dinner, the men would gather in the Billiard Room for a game. They'd smoke cigars and sip fine whiskey. Talk about their day's fishing. No women allowed." Her nose wrinkled when she winked at Dalton. "While the men went their way, the ladies would retire to the Piano Room for an evening of music and conversation. I think it will be the perfect spot for the show. Come see. I have the only key."

Shelby fumbled into her jacket's pocket and came out with a tarnished brass oval nearly the size of her hand. Attached to the brass was a length of chain, maybe a foot long, and hanging from the end of the chain was a single shiny silver key. She let the chain and brass dangle as she slipped the key into the lock.

"This is one of the rooms that are supposed to be haunted, isn't it?" Porsche moved closer to the door.

Shelby winked at me this time. "Our night clerks believe our founder's wife's ghost has been heard playing the piano on some late, late nights."

"Perfect," Porsche purred.

Shelby unlocked the door and showed us in. A grand piano sat in the middle of the room. Eddies of falling snow twirled outside the front windows. Windows on the side looked out over the gazebo and the pine tree where I had found Odyssey's rabbit. The pale floral wallpaper was a design that the founder's wife could have chosen in 1909.

From the lobby, a bellman knocked on the open door. "Message for Ms. Hurt." He held out a slip of paper.

"This room is just like you described. This is fabulous, Shelby." Porsche took the note and opened it. Her smile left. "Oh, no. Stephen King promised to be here for the show. He already owns two of Odyssey's paintings. Because of the storm, he's not sure if he'll be on time."

"Flight's delayed?" Shelby asked.

"Oh, no. Mr. King prefers not to fly. He and his wife are driving. He'll try to get here tomorrow, but he doubts if he'll make it at all." Her face turned little-girl pouty.

But I wasn't worried about whether the famous author would make it to Estes Park. I looked out the window toward the big pine tree. It was the same window where I had seen Jim Hayes watch me hide the headless rabbit. He ducked back when I saw him. If Shelby had the only key to the Piano Room, how did he get in there?

And why was he watching me?

Chapter 2

A sound like a slow hum vibrated from the glass in the windows. Gusting wind slapped the building, and a cascade of snow tumbled from the eaves. The feathery snowflakes of moments ago doubled in size and, instead of floating on the wind, the added moisture splattered the flakes against the glass.

Porsche trembled.

"Don't worry, ma'am, we can get some hellacious winds here in Estes. Air spills over those mountaintops and funnels down the canyons screamin' like a runaway train." It was Dalton. He took a sip of his coffee and added, "It's a mite early in the season for winds like there. Usually don't happen 'til later in the winter—January, February, March sometimes." He lowered his coffee cup and sucked the right end of his drooping mustache into the corner of his mouth and softly began to chew. "Somethin' just seems out of kilter this year."

"You're scaring her, Mr. Cummings." Shelby shot a glance my way.

I studied Dalton's face a moment more. I had learned to

read the man—who spoke few words—by his mustache. Chewing on the right side meant he was pondering something. When he chewed on the left, he was worried. The faster he chewed, the more worried he was.

The hum from the window glass rose two shrill notes, and I felt the world's kilter tilt.

No one said a word. The empty coffee cup hung uselessly in Dalton's gnarled hands. Shelby broke our little trance. She took Dalton's coffee cup and set it on the mantelpiece. She timed her words so we could hear between the window's rattles.

"Mr. Cummings and Hogan,"—she pointed—"this is the only other door to this room."

"Where's it go to?" Dalton asked.

"Here. Let me show you."

The knob turned in Shelby's hand. "That's strange. I thought the staff kept this locked. I'll be sure to ask someone," she said more to herself than to us. She then turned and smiled. It was a different smile. It was not quite like the practiced smile on the ghost tour leader's face, but it was close. Maybe Shelby had sensed the world tilt, too. "Anyway." She pointed to the door we had entered from the lobby. "Guests will come from there. Odyssey's pictures will be arranged on easels around the perimeter." She nodded to Porsche.

"Wonderful. I'll let Odyssey decide where she wants each canvas. We'll need to be in here later on tonight."

"Just let me know when," Shelby answered.

"Fine." Porsche scanned the room. I imagined her putting each piece of the show in place. She touched a long fingernail to her lips, then pointed. "I think I want security to stand there by the piano."

Dalton walked over and positioned himself beside the grand piano near the hinged side of the open lid. He turned to check his sight lines of the room. "We can do that."

"You will be armed?"

"Yes, ma'am. It's in the contract. Hogan and me got guns

and holsters."

"Good. It will add a certain tenseness to the gathering."

Tenseness. My stomach fell, and Dalton sucked the end of his mustache into his lips. The left side.

Porsche beamed at Dalton's answer. "And the refreshments?"

"Wine and cheeses. Our staff will serve guests on trays. Black dresses and starched white aprons," Shelby told her.

Porsche flipped her fingers. "I'll want to review the wine choices later. And I hope you've chosen younger women as servers. I wouldn't want some crone..."

"How, uh," I interrupted, "will the wine and cheese get to the room?"

"Through this door." Shelby swung the second door open. "There's a passageway around the men's billiard room to the kitchens. We use this when these rooms are needed for event seating." She reached inside the dark room and found a light switch.

The room was as long as the Piano Room but far narrower. No grand piano would fit inside. The wood paneling was dark oak. Against the far wall set a polished oak bar with empty wooden shelves, which I imagined once held only the finest, top-shelf whiskies and liquors. I could smell decades-old cigar smoke, and I was sure that if I listened closely enough, I'd hear the click of pool balls from the next room and a ghost's whispered curse at a missed shot.

"When Odyssey's paintings arrive, staff will bring them to this room. You'll be able to uncrate them in here and move them into the Piano Room for the display and auction," Shelby explained.

"I don't know if I like this," Porsche yawned. "It's so dark."

Shelby smiled. "I'll make arrangements for more lighting." She glanced my way and winked. "Come, I want you to see the Billiard Room. When this hotel opened, billiards was quite popular. This was billiards, not pool. Pool was played in the back of smoky saloons. Gentlemen played billiards." She smiled at me again. I enjoyed it. "The hotel's founder made sure that the tables were of the finest. I believe they were imported from France. The balls were carved from ivory and were quite fragile. The subfloors in this room were covered with cork and then a thick carpet in case an errant shot sent a ball off the table."

"I've seen enough." Porsche yawned again. "Let's go back to the lobby. It's too dingy in here. I need to check on the truck with Odyssey's paintings, and I need a drink."

Chapter 3

The logs in the lobby fireplace crackled, and a pop sent sparks onto the hardwood. Jim Hayes smashed the glowing orange spots under the sole of his shoe. Snow swirled outside the windows. Nests of wet flakes piled in the corners at the bottom of the window frames.

The next gust of wind sent a taste of smoke down the chimney. A line of guests waiting to check out turned as one when the great front door slammed shut. Nylon rustled on nylon and chubby thighs. Ms. Randolph led a line of six swishing, bright nylon-clad, gray-haired ladies from the open elevator to the windows to marvel at the falling snow.

Dalton and Shelby were at the front desk. She had the lobby phone to her ear, and Dalton had found his second cup of coffee. I drifted to the fireplace, hoping to warm my doubts about portraits of ghosts and ghouls.

The dour-faced tour leader had Hayes's attention. "It's not fair. No one thought of me." His teeth clenched, and the vein in the center of his forehead pulsed purple. "One tour this morning with *them*. Not one of them tipped. Not even a dollar." He tilted his head toward Ms. Randolph and the other ladies. "One tour tonight for the dignitaries." His voice sighed in displeasure. "Nothing tomorrow. Halloween is my busiest day of the year. Last year, I made over five hundred dollars in tips alone. This year, nothing. I count on that money. It's not fair."

I felt guilty for listening, but moved closer.

"Listen, Mr. Brown," Hayes whispered.

"Don't tell me to listen." The veins in his forehead pulsed faster.

"I didn't mean it like that." Hayes was practiced at calming the disgruntled, I could tell. "I'll talk to the management. Maybe we can work something out."

"Maybe." Brown trembled. His voice rose. "When have they ever thought about the people that make this what—"

Hayes stepped closer. "Lower your voice."

Brown fidgeted. He glanced around the room. Faces looked back. His shoulders dropped, and in that instant, he seemed two inches smaller.

Hayes edged even closer and whispered, "Get yourself a nice lunch. I'll tell the restaurant to charge it to the hotel. I'll have one of the ladies from housekeeping bring you the key to a vacant room. You can rest until your evening tour. Watch a football game. Take a nap. Whatever. If the weather stays like this," he nodded at the snow outside, "you can spend the night. No sense driving in this."

"I have to feed my cat," Brown whispered.

"You told me you set out food and water. He'll be okay for one night."

"She. My cat's a female."

"She'll be okay. You can drive home early. When the roads are plowed."

"Promise me you'll talk to management?" Brown's hooded eyes put a question mark on his question.

"I promise. Now, go on. Get something to eat. It's on us."

Hayes added another log to the fireplace. "Sorry you had to hear that."

"I only heard bits and pieces," I lied.

"A lot of the staff are complaining. Because of the art show, Ms. Hurt asked management to cut back on things like the ghost tours. Even the number of rooms. They're not renting rooms on the fourth floor at all."

"Can they afford to do that?"

"The gossip is that Ms. Hurt promised them fifteen percent of the art auction gross. She said that they have bids in hand for nearly a million now. That girl's paintings might sell for as much as twice that. You know what that means?"

I did the math. Fifteen percent of two million. "Three hundred thousand."

"Right to the bottom line." Hayes shook his head. "And Brown and the other staff? Bupcus."

The tallest in Ms. Randolph's group crossed the lobby to Hayes. Instead of nylon, her jogging suit was dark pink velour. Instead of the rustle of nylon on nylon, fabric on fabric made a brushing sound.

Jim Hayes snapped his shoulders back. "Is there something I can do for you, Miss Periwinkle?"

"That woman," she said.

I heard a trace of British in her voice.

"Ma'am, I'm not sure I understand." His ears perked.

"*Ms. Randolph.* If she tells me once more that she owns two of Odyssey's paintings, I might have to strangle her." Her eyes flamed, and for that instant, I could feel her fingers on my throat. She fumbled with a large diamond ring on one of her fingers and went on. "I need you to see to it that she is kept as far away from me as you can muster. Am I clear?"

Hayes was quick. "I'll talk to the event's liaison. I'll ask her to rearrange the dinner seating."

"The auction." Miss Periwinkle's eyes narrowed. "Make sure we are as far apart as you can make us. I intend to be sure she leaves here *without* another of Odyssey's paintings." There were daggers in the way she said it. "Now, excuse me."

I waited a long moment and then asked, "Miss Periwinkle?"

"Owns an art gallery in London. Came all that way for the suction."

—

I joined Dalton and Shelby at the end of the front desk. Shelby nodded and tipped her head to an empty place in the lobby. We took the hint and followed her.

"We needed to get away from the desk." She nodded at the line of people and luggage at the front desk. "Some want to get out before this storm gets worse. But most want to extend for another night." The faint freckles on her nose wrinkled, and she sighed. "We're booked solid. Poor girls. It's no fun to have to turn guests away. It's getting tense over there."

"Hayes just told me that the hotel's not using rooms on the fourth floor because of the art show."

She nodded. "That's what we've been told."

Dalton gulped the last of his coffee. "Thought you were in charge of the show."

"Just all the arrangements. This time, management handled the financial parts." Shelby shrugged. "Which reminds me. Porsche asked if one of you could be there when she and Odyssey hang the pictures. They plan on doing that sometime after midnight."

Dalton fumbled with his coffee cup. "Hogan will be there." And he left us.

"Who else is helping?" I asked.

"Jim Hayes arranged to open the crates and stage them in the Billiard Room. Just you, me, Porsche, and Odyssey will place the paintings. Can I ask that you not mention this to anyone?" Shelby's eyes made it an order. "Porsche is very concerned that some of Odyssey's fans might try to get an early peek at the paintings."

I nodded. "What about Porsche? She seemed a little shook about the—you know—*image*."

Shelby's nose wrinkled again. "I think it's everything she has going right now. She went to her room to *freshen*." Porsche might need to freshen up. Women like Shelby didn't. "She wants to meet with me for lunch to go over things." She shrugged her shoulders, and I felt guilty for enjoying what I saw.

Dalton came back with a fresh cup of coffee. "C'mon, Hogan. Truck's gonna be here any time now.

—

Dalton pressed a button mounted on the wall, and the dock door strained on its cables and began to move. Snowflakes swirled in as it opened, and cold air wrapped around us. Clouds of mist, as white as his mustache, drifted from Dalton's nostrils.

Outside, an engine groaned. Gears ground on metal. The engine revved and then went quiet.

I squinted out the loading dock door and then glanced at my watch. It was twenty after one, but the sky was as dark as evening, and white flakes, as thick as swarms of summer mosquitoes, danced in the whirl of wind off the building.

The engine came to life again. The gears strained. A bit of red tint from taillights cut through the gloom.

"I don't like it, Dalton. It's pretty steep downhill to this dock. As slick as it is, I don't know if he'll be able to get out."

"That'll be his problem. We got enough of our own to worry about."

Dalton leaned out the door and motioned to the driver to straighten out. Gears clanked. The truck edged forward a few feet and then backed. The rear tires caught the incline and began to spin on a slick layer of new ice. The truck rocked toward us.

"Slow down," Dalton hollered.

We jumped back, and with a thud that shook the doorframe

and the concrete under our feet, the truck slammed into the set of bald tires that cushioned the dock. The engine stalled, and a dark haze of exhaust smoke belched into the air. I choked, and Dalton waved a hand in front of his face.

"Damn hotrodder," he said.

Dalton took a fifty-cent package of Bull Durham from a coat pocket and fished papers from the bag. He shook the tobacco into the fold, twisted the packet, and licked the edge to seal things. A kitchen match appeared from his vest pocket, and he struck the match with his thumbnail. He sucked the flame into the paper, and smoke from his lungs blended into a twirl of snowflakes around the back end of the truck and the open door.

A face showed itself. It was armpit-high on the dock and stood beside the truck. The red glow from the taillights made the driver's face pinkish. He grabbed the corner of his truck and jumped up onto the dock. Braided hair on each side of his face fell to his shoulders. He hadn't shaved in a week. Despite the cold, he wore only a dirty T-shirt and dirtier jeans.

He eyed Dalton's cigarette and said, "If that's a doobie, can have a hit."

Dalton looked at me. The right corner of his mustache disappeared between his lips, and he began to chew. "Doobie? Hit?" He looked at me.

"He's talkin' about marijuana, boss. I'm sure he's jokin'"

The driver stuck out his hand to Dalton. "I'm Tad Slate. Sorry to be late, but the roads are a mess. That wet snow and the cold slicked things up. I bet there were a dozen cars in the ditch 'tween here and Drake." Tad Slate nodded at me. "I wasn't jokin' about a hit on that doobie."

"Dalton rolls his own. Cigarettes, that is."

"Goes with the hat, huh?" Tad pointed at Dalton's Stetson, then mocked, "Let's get this here rodeo a goin'. We got a truck to unload so I can get on down the hill."

The driver rolled up the door and stepped over a line of frozen slush into his truck. He pulled sheets of paper from his back pocket. "Says here we got twelve three-by-four crates, two four-by-fours, and a big mother back there. Four by eight. And it's heavy, too."

"We're here to help." Jim Hayes stepped off the stairway. Behind him stood three men in gray uniform shirts. The word "housekeeping" was embroidered over their chest pockets. "We'll stage the crates here and move them upstairs later. That's what Porsche wants."

Porsche? Hayes called the women Ms.—Ms. Randolph, Ms. Periwinkle. Never by a first name. Was it a slip, or—

Chapter 4

Jim Hayes's blazer hung from a doorknob. His tie was tucked into the front of his shirt, and he'd rolled his sleeves up to his elbows. Circles of sweat looped his armpits. "That's the last one," he said and stepped back from the largest crate. One side of his shirttail had pulled free, and a roll of hairy belly hung over his belt.

Dalton hung a hip on one of the smaller boxes. He peeled off his goatskin gloves and smacked the dust from the knees of his jeans. "That sumabitch wasn't that heavy. Just awkward. How you reckon they got on the truck?"

"It's off now, and that's all I care about." It was Tad Slate, the truck driver. His Willie Nelson pigtails wagged as he shook his head. He grabbed the strap that dangled from the door of his truck and tugged at it. Sheets of slushy snow catapulted onto the edge of the dock as the door snapped closed. Slate stepped back. "Double-check me. But I marked off each piece as it came off. They're all here. Fifteen pieces. No damage either. Sign it and let me get out of here."

Dalton stepped around the largest crate and took the weigh bill from Slate. He handed it to Hayes. "See this here?" He smacked the side of the crate with his gloves. Bright orange letters had been stenciled on the rough plywood. He read the words out loud. "This crate is to be opened *only* by Odyssey Pruit."

He turned to me. "Odyssey?" His face showed disgust. "She's the one who painted all these?" His eyes counted the other crates that crowded the room.

"It's her money that pays our bill," I reminded him.

"Pfft." He blew through his mustache and stepped back from the chill through the open door. "Sign his papers and send him on his way, Hayes."

A black wall phone near the door jangled. Hayes picked up the receiver and tucked it between his ear and shoulder while he scribbled on Slate's papers. "We're finishing up down here. I'll come up as soon as I can," he said into the phone.

Slate took the papers and jammed them in his back pocket. He nodded to Dalton and me, and he slipped through the opening between the doorframe and his truck. A string of curses followed, then, "Snow's up over my knees." The driver-side door creaked and slammed shut. The engine sputtered and then took hold. Dark exhausted belched into the room and stung my eyes.

I stuck my head out of the opening. Thick flakes pelted the top of my head. The driver's door opened and Slate leaned out and swept the snow from the windshield with his bare arm. Back inside, he revved the engine and slipped the truck into low gear.

The truck jerked forward a few inches, and the tires lost their grip and began to spin. Chunks of dirty snow and bits of ice rocketed into the air.

Curse words I hadn't heard since the army penetrated the glass and sheet metal of the truck's cab. Slate pounded a fist on the steering wheel, and another string of words questioned the ancestry of his truck.

"I was afraid that might happen," Dalton said, and then added to me, "Shouldn't have tried it in the first place."

Slate was at the door. "I'm stuck."

Dalton tipped his hat forward and motioned to the three workers. "Let's figure out how to get him unstuck."

Hayes raised a hand to us. He nodded as if the person on the other end of the phone line could see his agreement. He mumbled, "Yes, ma'am. I'm on my way," and hung up. "I'm needed upstairs."

"Go on. We can monkey with his. Won't need your help." Dalton zipped up his jacket and stuffed his hands into his gloves.

"But Ms. Hurt is requesting that one of the security team come with me."

"Say what it was about?"

"No, but the hotel manager sounded—" He paused as if he were searching for the correct word. Finally, "Tense."

"Hogan, you go with him," Dalton said. "I'm better with stuck trucks than I am talking to women."

My guts knotted. Something told me I should stay and push the truck.

—

Hayes and I threaded our way around the stacked crates and through a door into the next room.

"Where's that go?" I nodded down a shadowy basement corridor.

"We bring shipments in from the loading dock. There's a freight elevator at the end there." He pointed. "One floor up is the kitchen, and the floor above that is where housekeeping keeps its supplies. The old man gave it some thought when he designed his place."

"Is that the way we'll take the crates to the Piano Room?"

"No, there's another elevator that way." He waved his hand. "A dumbwaiter, really. A narrow stairway, too. That's how they kept the bar by the Billiard Room well stocked." Hayes grinned. "Legend says that while the wives were in the Piano Room next door, ladies of negotiable virtue could be ushered up the back stairway." He gave a wink. "The founder thought of everything. C'mon, follow me."

—

The hair on the top of my head brushed the ceiling. My shoulder touched the wall. "Tight fit," I said, and scrunched my neck down a bit more.

"They never guessed that people in 1982 would be taller and wider than men in 1909." Hayes flipped a switch, and bare light bulbs, maybe eight feet apart, flickered on above the narrow stairs. "That's the dumbwaiter there." He pointed. "The platform is big enough to hold four kegs of beer. You raise it with a chain and pulley system. Ingenious really. We won't have any trouble with those smaller crates." He started up the stairs. "Watch your head."

I tucked tighter into my collar and followed.

"The last bartender, who worked the Billiard Room, told his liquor runners if they didn't have at least three bumps on the top of their heads, they weren't working hard enough," Hayes said it like he was trying to amuse one of the hotel's guests. "Twenty-one steps to the top, Hogan. It's better if you count them."

When he reached step number seven on the narrow stairs, his chest and shoulders all but blocked the dim light from the bare bulbs. Shadows darkened. When I looked down, I couldn't see my feet. That's why Hayes said to count the steps. We moved three steps higher, and the texture of the darkness around me changed. It collected between my fingers and spread over my face until it turned sticky like old pancake syrup.

Hayes huffed for his next breath. The wooden stairs underneath him groaned. Stair ten of twenty-one, I guessed.

"Feel that? They never saw the need for heat on these stairs.

You could see your breath if it wasn't so dark. Even on the hottest days of the summer and it's still cool in here." Hayes hadn't moved. "Remember, I told you about the ladies of the night that were smuggled up these stairs? One of the legends of this old place has it that a proper wife in the Piano Room found out what was going on and chased one of the chippies to these stairs. The whore slipped and fell down the dumbwaiter shaft. Broke her neck. It's her cold breath you feel now."

"Yeah, right," I said. But the stickiness between my fingers chilled, and goosebumps ran up my arms.

The stairs under Hayes creaked again, and he began to climb. Sixteen I counted, and more light seeped in around Hayes's shadow. Hayes made the top, and I hurried the last five steps.

"I felt like a kid who found a secret passage." I tried smiling to warm the chill.

"Oh, this old hotel has several more, and all are just as uninviting. But they can be a big help sometimes." Hayes's face was flushed. He struggled for his next breath. "Steep, wasn't it?" he wheezed. He put a hand on the wall to steady himself. "I need a minute."

I looked around the narrow landing at the top of the stairs. Dust and fine spiderwebs collected on maybe two dozen photographs thumbtacked to the wall. "What's this?" I asked.

"Sometime in the early 1950s, the hotel staff started a tradition. At the end of summer, they'd gather kitchen help, maids, maintenance, desk clerks, bartenders, waitresses, and the whole lot for a picnic. Gave everyone a chance to drink beer and bitch about management and rude guests. Mainly, they drank beer. Somebody had the idea of taking a group picture. Did the same the next year and the year after that. Someone thought this was a good place to hang them. Later on, management liked the idea and in 1975 they hired a professional photographer. Those pictures are in the general manager's office. The old ones are still here. No particular order. If you look close, some of the very first ones are snapshots taken with a Kodak Brownie. I'm in a couple of the newer ones."

I leaned in. The corners of some of the pictures curled, and images faded. Some were black and white. The newer ones were in color. "When did you start here?"

"Fifty-seven. Right out of high school. Mowed the lawns and picked up trash that first year. Next, I washed the bedding. Then I made bellboy. Just the summers then. I thought I was I ski bum. Took off in the winter to work the ski lifts and sell tow tickets in places like Breckenridge and Aspen. Made the ski patrol some years. Broke an ankle in sixty-eight. Talked a little hippy girl into following me back here that summer. She moved on by August, and I've been here ever since."

"You must like it."

Hayes didn't answer.

I looked back at the snapshots. In a picture near the center, I could make out a much younger, much slimmer Jim Hayes. There was a longneck Coors in his fist. His smile was a snarl, and the young Jim didn't look as worn out as this Jim.

Hayes absently straightened his tie. A comb appeared from his blazer's pocket, and he ran it through his thinning hair, then swept the dust from his jacket with his fingers. "Come with me."

The narrow passage opened into the Billiard Room. Hayes fumbled for a key and unlocked the lobby door. Warmth greeted us. Hayes straightened a bit as he stepped out. "Returning guest over there. He comes almost every year. Some years, more than once. Always insists I help him." Hayes's lobby face returned. "I see he has his new wife with him. She would be number four." Brisk steps took him to the couple waiting by the fireplace.

Steel-gray hair showed under the man's cowboy hat. A silver bolo tie hung over a dark shirt, and he was wearing a new ski coat that had to cost as much as Dalton's pickup. Mrs. Number Four tapped a toe on the hardwood. I couldn't tell how old she was. But her outfit cost more than his jacket, maybe two times more, and she was practiced at being disinterested.

"Doctor Kane," I heard Hayes say.

"Call me Everett, Jim. You know that," Doctor Kane snaked his arm around his fourth wife's slender waist. She stiffened. "And I'd like you to meet my wife, Sugar. I've told her so much about this old hotel."

Hayes tipped his head to the woman. She ignored him. "How was your drive?"

"Treacherous," the doctor answered. "I was determined to get here. Gave Sugar a bit of a scare. Cars in the ditch everywhere you looked. We were one of the last ones through. State Patrol closed the road at the mouth of the canyon. We heard on the radio that the governor declared a state of emergency. I guess the airport in Denver shut down. I-25 is an icy mess. This storm is supposed to last through the weekend."

I looked around the lobby. It was almost empty. None of the commotion of earlier. Ms. Randolph and the nylon ladies staked out chairs near the window and were enjoying the snow outside. The fire in the fireplace was dying. Only one clerk leaned on the lobby counter. A clock somewhere chimed three times.

Just then, every light flickered and then went out.

"Now this, too?" Sugar Kane's foot tapped on the floor.

Chapter 5

No one in the lobby spoke. The tapping of shoe leather on hardwood was the only sound. Outside, the three o'clock sky was the color of tarnished pewter. Blizzard-driven snowflakes sliced the air like primal spirits fleeing everything evil.

One grain at a time, my eyes separated shapes from shadows. Ms. Randolph and the other ladies stood at the front window. They whispered to one another about the storm.

In the red glow from the fireplace's dying embers, Doctor Kane reached for Sugar. She stiffened. He leaned closer and took her hands in his. "It's beautiful," he said softly and pulled her to him. The tap of her shoe quickened.

The woman behind the registration desk gripped the counter's edge with both hands. When another shape joined her from the back office, she leaned her head on the newcomer's shoulder.

Jim Hayes's silhouette crossed the lobby, backlit by the ghostly, greenish tint of an exit sign. He fumbled with a panel on the wall next to the stone fireplace. The door creaked open. Hayes reached inside. There was a clunk of metal on wood. Then, a flashlight beam bored a tunnel through the dark lobby. People turned, and sets of eyes became pinkish spots against the gray shadows.

The quiet grew louder. Each muscle in my body cringed. I searched the corners for the ghosts in Odyssey's paintings. Then, scolded myself for looking.

"Everything is all right," Jim Hayes's voice filled the room. It was calm and forceful, not loud at all. "This sort of thing can happen with these kinds of storms. I'm sure they will have it fixed in a few minutes. A half-hour at the most. If not, the hotel has backup generators—"

"Look. See it?" Ms. Randolph squeaked. "Out there in the distance. It wasn't there before. It was dark, like everything else."

"I see it." There was a clunk from the window glass as one of Ms. Randolph's companions pointed a finger.

I crossed the lobby and gazed out the window over the women. Far off against the gray sky and flutter of snowflakes, a pinpoint of yellow light shone. Closer to us, another splash of light came alive.

As one, the ladies sighed.

I sensed the doctor and Sugar move closer. Jim Hayes doused his flashlight and edged up to the other side of the window. The women from the registration desk were there, too. Other guests crowded in.

Down the hill, the streetlights and storefronts along the town's main street burst on like a fireworks display. On the hill above the town, lights in living rooms and bedrooms flickered on. A gust of wind stronger than all the others rattled the windows. The swirl of flakes outside became a twisting, angry tornado of white.

The whole hotel groaned.

In that second, the lights all around us came on. Darkness,

shadows, and Odyssey's spirits fled. I had to squint in the new brightness.

"There, I told you it would be all right," Jim Hayes said.

—

A little girl peeked around the open door of the Cascades Restaurant. Her blonde hair was swept away from her face and pulled into a long ponytail. Her dress was blue. It hung below her knees with short white sleeves that seemed more fit for summer than a night of snow and blizzards. She was barefoot.

I remembered my girls when they were that age and the many arguments over the child's choice of what to wear. Many times, Jenny decided other battles were more important. Perhaps this mother had given in also.

"It's okay. The lights are back on," I told her.

She tilted her head, smiled at me, and whirled away.

Perhaps, twenty tables in the dining room. Starched white tablecloths covered each, and candles flickered through the leaded glass lanterns at the center of the table. Tented linen napkins sat on the plates, and the silver service shone.

Shelby and Porsche shared a table under the windows. Porsche stared absently out at the snow. A large leather handbag sat at her feet. She held a half-filled wineglass.

A couple with a little boy, about the same age as the girl, sat at a table near the center of the room. The boy held a hamburger with both hands. He was maybe ten. His father jostled his son's hair. The mother stared at the snow outside and picked at a salad.

Miss Periwinkle was alone near the opposite wall. An empty martini glass sat on her table. A full one was in her hand. I nodded to her as I crossed the room. Her eyes watched, but she made no effort to acknowledge me.

Cloudy images scrolled across the screen of a black-and-white TV hung in the corner of the shelves behind the bar. One bar stool was taken. The man wore work boots, jeans, and a down vest over a flannel shirt. He nursed a beer.

The bartender set two drinks on a tray next to two others. All were doubles. He waved to the lone waitress. She took the tray to a table at the back.

I looked for the barefoot girl in the blue summer dress. She wasn't there. With my next step, a cold draft, like someone had dared to open a window, wrapped around me.

Shelby motioned for me to join them. I slipped into a chair beside her.

Porsche turned from the window. Red rimmed her eyes, and her makeup was smeared. "I don't know how I can tell Odyssey all this. She'll be crushed.

"The storm, you mean?"

Shelby touched my hand. "In the last twenty minutes, we had some news…"

"Bad news," Porsche said. "Terrible news. We never thought…" A finger caught a tear at the corner of her eye.

Shelby signaled to the waitress as she passed. "Bring her another." She pointed to Porsche's wineglass. Shelby cleared her throat and turned to me. "This storm seems to have complicated—"

"Complicated, huh?" Porsche moaned. "Ruined is more like it."

Shelby went on. "The Denver airport is closed."

"I heard. Someone said the governor declared a state of emergency. Sounds like the eastern half of the state is locked down."

"Exactly. Most of Porsche's guests will not be able to get here."

Porsche touched an eye with the corner of a table napkin. "My office in New York called. Stephen King is stranded in Grand Island, Nebraska. Imagine. John Denver can't get out of Aspen. That new one. He just took over the late-night talk show, —David, uh?"

"Letterman?" I asked.

"Yeah, him. All flights to Denver are canceled." Porsche downed the last bit of wine from her glass. "Your Governor Lamm won't be here. What with the election just days away, he wanted to be seen in public. Even if he could make it, he's too busy with the storm."

A swish of nylon crossed the restaurant. The waitress showed Ms. Randolph and the other ladies to a table. Porsche feigned a smile and waved at the group. The ladies waved back, and Ms. Randolph tittered.

"How many were expected at the auction?"

"The event is by invitation only. Those ladies," Porsche tilted her head toward Ms. Randolph's group, "have each purchased at least one of Odyssey's works. They think of themselves as the ones who discovered her. They paid perhaps two hundred dollars for the early pictures. Now they are going for twenty times that. Only Ms. Randolph has the financial wherewithal to expect to win another at the auction."

"So, Ms. Randolph is rich?"

"Don't be fooled. She could buy and sell this hotel ten times over. Her husband's family are partners in twenty-some Hilton properties in New England. Among other things. And it's her late husband." Porsche waved again to the ladies.

I shot a glance across the room. "And Miss Periwinkle?"

"Stuffy, isn't she?" Porsche smiled and raised her wineglass. From her table, Miss Periwinkle tipped her head, raised a mostly empty martini glass, and returned Porsche's smile. "Delores Periwinkle and her domestic partner..." Porsche paused and pretended to sip her wine. I suspected it was to give me time to absorb what she had just said. "They own an exclusive gallery in London. She's here to try to snap up some things for resale."

"The same with the table in the back. On one side, you have brothers from Paris. Each owns a gallery. They came to Colorado to secure at least one of Odyssey's pieces. The men across the table are a father and son. Gallery in Madrid. They're here for the same reason. And what's best is that the two families hate each other. They're being cordial tonight. It will be fangs and claws when the bidding starts. You know how men can be. They sometimes feel compelled to show each other who has the biggest..." Porsche glanced at me. I squirmed. She finished the last drop of her wine. Then to Shelby, "I thought you asked the server to bring me another."

Shelby raised her hand. The waitress was at the bar. She nodded and said something bartender. He poured a glass of wine, and the waitress brought it to our table.

"So sorry." She set the glass near Porsche. "We're short on help. Roads are so bad that our waitstaff can't make it in."

As one, we turned to look out the windows. Flakes driven sideways all but blotted out the dark sky.

"Told the boss if he'd get me a room for the night, I'd work until closing tonight and help with the breakfast in the morning. He took me up on it."

"Porsche and Mr. Hogan, this is Claire," Shelby told us. "She has been at the hotel for almost twenty years."

"I've never seen a storm like this one. Most of the help left early, and I doubt the night shift even tried to make it in. There's just a cook and one helper in the kitchen. Good thing the hotel's only half full tonight." Tiredness showed in Claire's eyes. "Ah, crap," she mumbled. "More guests."

Doctor Kane and Sugar waited at the door. Claire signaled for them to pick a table and hurried off.

"Does Doctor Kane collect Odyssey's work?" I asked Porsche.

"No. At least not yet. He contacted me. Said this old hotel is one of his favorites and wanted to know if he could attend. Said it would be a honeymoon present for his wife." Porsche rolled her eyes. "I checked his financials myself. Doctor Kane is a retired pediatrician, and he's a partner in three shopping malls in Houston and two in San Antonio." She took a drink and, when set the glass down, asked, "Do I sound gossipy?"

"No, not at all," I lied. "One more thing, someone said that there are almost a million dollars in bids already." Shelby nudged me. I wondered if I should have asked and quickly added, "Am I out of place?"

The wine in Porsche's glass was nearly gone. "Who told you that?"

"I don't remember." A second lie.

"Let's just say a lot of money will change hands at the auction." Porsche reached into her handbag and handed me a slick booklet. "That's the catalog for the event. I had copies couriered to prospects. Michael Jackson..." Porsche paused. "Yes, that Michael Jackson. Has placed a bid. You might enjoy looking through the catalog. Suggested opening bids for each piece are listed below the pictures. Odyssey even painted a picture of this very room. I think it's on page eleven."

I thumbed through the pages and opened the catalog to page eleven. The picture was crude, almost childlike, but I recognized the bar and tables. Every detail seemed correct. A man and a woman shared the very table where we sat. He was eating a hamburger. She looked out the window. It was snowing.

Shelby touched the corner of the page so she could see better. Her fingers grazed mine. I looked at the page again. The cold draft I had felt when I crossed the room wrapped around me. I felt Shelby shiver.

In the picture of the restaurant, near the doorway where I had entered, a pale figure crouched. I looked closer. Somehow, Odyssey's brushstrokes made the paleness almost shine. It was a little girl. She was barefoot. She wore a blue dress with white short sleeves. The title of the portrait was *Betsy,* and the suggested opening bid was two hundred and fifty thousand dollars.

—

Porsche was lost in her third glass of wine. "Sigourney Weaver," she muttered. "I feel guilty for liking that movie." Her eyes were glazed. "Alien, silly," she giggled at me. "Did you see it?"

Shelby nudged my arm. "Sigourney Weaver canceled. Porsche was hoping to meet her."

"But Sigourney sent bids on three pieces." Porsche raised her empty wineglass to the waitress.

Claire nodded.

Shelby cleared her throat. She shook her head.

Claire stepped to the table. "Have you decided?" she asked with a smile. Claire's eyes met Shelby's. She mouthed, "I understand."

"The trout." Porsche rested her forehead in her hands. "Bring another glass—no, a bottle for the table."

Claire glanced at Shelby.

It was Shelby who mouthed something this time. The word was, "no."

Claire smiled, "For you, Shelby?"

"The soup. And get Mr. Hogan whatever he'd like." She looked at me. The freckles on her nose wrinkled. "It's on us."

Instead of looking at the menu, I nodded at the couple with their son. "I'll have a burger like the little boy." I didn't turn back to the waitress. I felt a bit guilty for how much I enjoyed looking at Shelby.

Porsche still stared at her glass. For an instant, I pretended it was just Shelby and me at the table. I wanted to say something clever. I wanted her to smile, and I needed her to laugh.

But doubts tumbled through my mind, and I said nothing.

Cold air wrapped around me again. Shelby felt it, too. I heard a child's giggle, but when I turned to look, the little boy's face rested on the table, and he was fast asleep.

I looked down at the open art catalog on the table. The picture was of this restaurant, and a little girl named Betsy peeked in from the doorway.

"No," I told myself, "don't even think it."

Dalton crossed the restaurant to our table. His Stetson hung from his fingers. Specks of moisture sparkled against the black felt on the brim. He set the hat on an adjoining table, crown down, pulled out a chair, and straddled it.

Porsche's face was in one hand, and her elbow rested on the table. She smiled at him.

Dalton shook his head and looked at me. "Hogan, you look like you've seen a ghost."

I needed to push Betsy far away. "Get the truck unstuck?" I asked.

"Pfft," Dalton blew through his mustache. "This storm is somethin'. We tried digging him out and spreading sand. The ramp was just too icy. The driver revved her up, and the wheels just spun. He wouldn't let up, and something gave away underneath with a clunk. Surprised you didn't hear it up here. Probably a U-joint. He ain't going nowhere."

"Call a tow truck?"

"Pfft," again, "Even if they could get up here, every tow truck in the state is busy pulling the stranded outta ditches. And I doubt they would even try to get here."

"What about the driver? What was his name?"

"Slate. Tad Slate. He's on the phone with his boss. Had his credit card in his hand and was asking about a room for the night. He was mumbling somethin' about bein' hungry. If he shows up in here, he ain't sittin' with us. There's somethin' about that pigtailed hippy sumabitch I just don't like." Dalton looked for a place to spit his tobacco. The starched linen and fine silver forbade him. Defeat was written on his face. Slowly, he moved the wad to the side of his cheek.

Porsche smiled at him.

Dalton shook his head. "Damn, that reminds me. I gotta find Hayes. Slate's truck ended up so close to the dock that we couldn't pull the door all the way down. Maybe six inches open is all. I stuffed a tarp along the opening. But the door won't latch. He should know."

Claire brought our food. "Something for you?" she asked

Dalton.

He eyed my burger. "I'll have what Hogan's havin'."

"And to drink?"

"Jack and Coke," he mumbled. "And hold the Coke."

Dalton left his hat on the table. "Be right back. I need to tell Hayes about that door."

Porsche picked at the food on her plate. She seemed deep in thought or drowsy from the wine. I couldn't tell.

The hotel clock struck once.

It was five-thirty.

Claire stopped at our table with Dalton's burger and a tumbler half full of amber liquid. She raised on her tiptoes and looked out the window. "I never remember a storm that came in so fast and hard. And so early in the year. There's already more than two feet out there. And the wind." The waitress shivered.

"It's supposed to last all night," Porsche mumbled.

"Poor Eva." Claire squeezed her hands together.

"Eva?"

Shelby touched my arm. I felt guilty for enjoying her touch. "Eva is a..." Shelby hesitated. Finally, she said, "I was going to say, friend. That's not exactly true. Eva's homeless. And I suspect a little,"—she touched the side of her head with two fingers—"you know, troubled. She finds her way to Estes every fall. The kitchen staff leaves a plate of food where she can find it almost every night. Right about this time." Shelby looked out the window. "Two weeks ago, they found her sleeping in one of the outbuildings where maintenance stores their mowers. They had to tell the sheriff. They took her to a shelter in Boulder. She was back in two days."

"I saw her downtown yesterday," Claire said. "She hangs out near the library on cold days." She looked out the window. "I hope she's all right."

"I'm sure she has a place to stay," I said, but I wasn't sure at all.

Dalton sat down at the table next to ours. He took a sip from the glass and held it in his mouth for a long time.

"Need some ketchup?" Claire asked.

He nodded.

"I'll get you some."

The food was good. The cold draft stayed away, and the room was as warm as Dalton's bourbon. We all held thoughts of the cold night and wondered about a woman named Eva. Falling snow spread shadows across the room, and the light from the candles on each table melted the shadows away.

"I need to check on Odyssey." Porsche stood. She reached out and steadied herself on a chair back.

Dalton mopped the last of his burger through a puddle of ketchup on his plate and stuffed it in his mouth with two fingers. "I'll go with you. Then I'll check things in the lobby and the Piano Room. Roam around a bit." He stood and took Porsche by the elbow and plucked his black hat from the table. "Hogan, I forgot to tell you, I brought your gear in from the truck. It's behind the front counter." And they left us.

I sat at the table with Shelby. Odyssey's paintings had arrived before the storm closed the roads. Porsche guests wouldn't make it, but they were safe. Those who were here at the hotel had rooms and food. The auction would go on. And the storm would break.

Sometime.

Outside, the wind howled. Snow swirled.

"Poor Eva," I thought.

I shut my eyes for a long moment.

When I opened them. Everything was black.

—

Table candles made the darkness dirty gray. People's gasps turned into soft words and nervous laughter. They turned to the windows. Outside, snowflakes, bigger than silver dollars, slashed the night sky. The wind moaned like a dentist's drill.

Sugar Kane held a drink the color of window glass cleaner,

to her lips. Waves of light from the candle turned her face garish blue. Her husband reached out to touch her.

Shelby stood and raised her voice to the room. "Folks, it's the storm again. Like before. I'm sure if we wait a few minutes, the power will come back on. Please bear with us."

All around us, the soft words went softer, and this time no one laughed.

It was so quiet I could hear silverware touching plates and the sound of lips on the rim of a glass.

Shelby bent down and whispered in my ear, "Finish your meal. I need to help Claire serve the food."

And the hotel clock struck seven times.

I felt Shelby's breath on my face. "But wait for me. Porsche said something—" It was barely a whisper. "I need to talk to you."

—

The candle on my table flickered its last, and a thread of pale smoke disappeared into the dark. I squinted at my watch. The pale luminance from the Rolex's hands and dial showed it was ten minutes to eight. Except for candlelight and the glow of an exit sign, the dining room had been dark for nearly an hour.

I played with the last French fry on the plate, pretending it was a ship sailing through an ocean of dark ketchup. My eyes had tried to adjust to the dark, but only painted everything in shades of gray and black. From the lobby, the flames in the fireplace reflected in blurred yellows and oranges on the front window glass.

"Hogan." It was Dalton's hoarse whisper.

I wondered why people whispered in the dark. Could one only speak out loud in the light?

"Hogan."

Dalton and Jim Hayes waited in the tinge of green from the exit sign. Dalton motioned for me to join them. I checked for Shelby in the shadows. She disappeared through the kitchen door.

I picked my way around the tables. Not one guest had moved since the power went off, and I took a deep breath when I passed the place where the little girl in blue had smiled at me.

"Gonna need your help," Dalton whispered. "Just got off the phone with the state police. Tell 'em what they said, Hayes."

Hayes rubbed his mouth. "We won't have power at least 'til morning. If then. It's a real mess out there. Crews are out, but I guess when they get something up and working, another stretch somewhere else goes down. Nobody was prepared for this." He nodded toward the hotel's front door. "We still have phone service for now. Chances are good we could lose it, too."

"Tell 'em 'bout the roads," Dalton huffed.

"Closed." Hayes shook his head. The shadows turned his face pale.

"All of them?"

"That's what it sounds like. Boulder, Longmont, Loveland, Fort Collins, and Greeley, too, have all put a shelter at home law in effect. No one except emergency vehicles is on the roads. The governor called out the National Guard to shuttle doctors and nurses to the hospitals. I-25 is shut down from Colorado Springs to Wheatland, Wyoming. I-70 is closed from the Kansas line to Denver, and nothing is moving west at all." Hayes finally took a breath. "As bad as it is here, Vail has almost three feet of snow, and it's still coming down."

"Pfft, them poor millionaires," Dalton huffed.

"You said something about the hotel's backup generators."

"They kicked in about half an hour ago." Hayes brought his fist to his mouth and tapped his lips three times. "It's not much of a system. They got some light in the kitchen. The refrigerators and freezers stay on. There are lights on the stair landings and a bulb at the end of each hallway on the second and third floors. Nothing on the fourth."

"But you said, no one is staying on the fourth?"

"Pfft. You and me," Dalton groused.

"You two and we put a few of the staff who have agreed to stay and help out up there. You'll need to use flashlights."

I glanced back into the restaurant. People still sat at their tables. Candles flickered.

I pointed. "Does the restaurant have any more of those candles?"

"Maybe a few." Hayes gathered his thoughts.

"Something is bothering me." I shifted from one foot to the other. "Do we know for sure how many people are in the hotel right now?"

Hayes thought. "I couldn't tell you. But, but—I'll have one of the girls at the front desk go through the check-ins. We can get a count that way."

I followed Hayes and Dalton out into the lobby. Hayes leaned over the registration counter and whispered to the woman in the dark, "Hogan will bring you some candles from the kitchen. I want you to..." and he explained about the guest count.

Hayes loosened his tie. "You know, we keep three or four dozen flashlights under the counter in case something like this happens." He reached under the counter and came out with a box. "And I've got probably a dozen more in my cabinet by the fireplace. They're the cheap plastic kind." He held one up. "Batteries don't last that long, and if you drop 'em on the hard floor, they'll shatter like glass, but they'll do for now. We can share them with the guests."

"I'll take some to the kitchen for Shelby and the rest."

He handed me six flashlights, and he stuffed three more in his jacket's pocket. "I'll find those guys from housekeeping. They can start moving the paintings upstairs to the Piano Room. That dumbwaiter I showed you works fine. All they have to do is pull the chain."

I thought for a moment. "Is that wise? I mean, there are no lights."

"They can be careful. I trust them. I'll tell them to do the best they can."

His hand found the lobby phone on the counter. He picked the black receiver.

Even in the dark, I could sense his face growing pale. "It's dead," he whispered.

"So, we're on our own."

Chapter 6

I stepped out of the dark dining room into the kitchen. Outside, snow spilled from the windowsill, and frost sparkled in lazy triangles at the corners of the glass. A single light fixture over the work area chased shadows into the room's edges. The chef stood at a gas range. Things sizzled, and steam bubbled from the pots. He stirred, moved long-handled skillets from one burner to the next, sprinkled ingredients into simmering pans, and stirred the pots while his helper prepared the plates.

Shelby had slipped a white chef's coat over her blouse and skirt. Her thick caramel-colored ponytail was secured in a hairnet. She grabbed a pair of potholders and slid a large flat pan into the oven.

I sniffed the air. "Cookies?"

As she turned, Shelby pulled the hair net loose and held it behind her back.

"Oatmeal." She smiled. "There's a batch of chocolate chip cooling over there. You stay away from them, Guy Hogan."

She hadn't used my first name before. I liked the way it

sounded.

The freckles on her nose wrinkled. "If there's time, I'll mix up some peanut butter next."

"Time?"

"I had an idea. Last spring, a thunderstorm knocked out the power, and we invited our guests to come to the lobby. Some of the staff shared stories about the hotel. We ate cookies and popcorn. Someone had a guitar. It kept them entertained and happy until the rain stopped and the power came back on."

"You'd better make a lot of cookies."

Her smile faded. "What do you mean?"

"Hayes talked with the state police. We might not have power back until sometime tomorrow morning."

"It's that bad?"

"Yeah. Roads closed. Nothing moving. Sounds like most of the state's locked down. They're not expecting the storm to break for twenty-four hours. If then."

She nodded. "We'll make more cookies. I had Claire tell the ladies at the front desk to spread the word. Those who want to can gather in the lobby in half an hour. We're closing the kitchen, but the chef is going to make some popcorn. I mean, he's stuck here like the rest of us."

We both gazed at the swirl of snow outside.

"It's the worst I can remember."

"Is it really? Bad, I mean." She brushed a strand of hair from her face. "Or is it just a reminder of how small we are? What is it they say? Men make plans and God laughs." Shelby dropped the hairnet on the table. "Anyway?"

"Here," I laid the flashlights beside her hairnet. "We'll give some to the guests. These are for the kitchen. Hayes said don't drop them, or that cheap plastic will break." I leaned closer. "You said there was something you wanted to tell me."

Shelby picked up a flashlight but didn't turn it on. Even in the shadowy kitchen, her face darkened. "It's Odyssey. Next time you see her, look at her neck." Shelby tilted her head back and touched her throat. "Please look."

"What?"

A gust of air, as cold as the breath from the lungs of a little girl ghost, funneled through the kitchen and wrapped around us. Then the wind slammed a door shut.

"Shelby." Claire hurried to where we stood. Drops of melting snow turned her gray hair silver. "The plate. It's gone." Tears cracked her voice.

"What plate?" Shelby took Claire by the arm and pulled her close.

"Even though you told me not to, I had the chef put a plate together—for Eva. I thought—you know what I thought—I set it outside a while ago. It's gone. She must have taken it. And she's out there in this storm. She'll freeze if she hasn't already." Claire held back a sob. "We need to help her."

"Are you sure about the plate?" I asked. "Maybe the snow covered it. I can't imagine she'd be out in this storm.

"No. I went out there to check. It's not there."

The two women followed me to the door. I shone one of Hayes's flashlights through the window. I could see the smudges of Claire's footprints. In those seconds, the blizzard took control, and her footprints all but disappeared.

—

"I'll take a look," Dalton said. "Brought in my heavy coat and winter boots. You don't have anything but that sweater and jacket, Hogan."

"But you shouldn't go out there alone."

Dalton reached behind the hotel's counter and grabbed his duffel bag. "Hold this." He handed me a flashlight. His was heavy metal, not plastic. "Shine it on my bag." He pulled out a hooded parka, gloves, and a wool cap. He sat down on a straight-backed chair, struggled out of his cowboy boots, and slipped his feet into a pair of insulated Sorel work boots.

"I don't think you should go out there by yourself, Mr.

Cummings," Shelby said. "It's cold, and the wind is terrible."

"She's right, Dalton. Where's Hayes?"

"He went on downstairs with those three bellboys to start moving those pictures. And I know what I'm doin'."

"Still, Dalton?"

The old game warden shook his head. "I done stuff like this before. Tell ya what. All I'll do is walk along the side of the building. You'll be able to watch me from the window. I'll see if I can find any sign the woman's been here." He grunted and pulled the laces tight on the heavy boots. "If I find something, I'll decide then what to do next. I'm too old to play hero. All we need now is to find out if she's out there in this snow." He stood up and slipped his arms into his coat.

"Hey there, can I help?" Tad Slate stood up from the shadows on the stairs. "I heard you talkin'. I got my heavy coat. Boots, too. Who we lookin' for?"

"What were you doing there?" Shelby asked. "Hiding?"

"No, ma'am." Slate stepped into the circle of light from Dalton's flashlight. "I was waiting to get me a room. I heard that sometimes hotels will cut you a break if they have empty rooms and you check in just before they close. That's all."

"So, you were just sitting there in the dark?"

"Yes, sir. I do that a lot."

Shelby's fingers touched my arm. An uneasiness crept up from my stomach.

Dalton stood and huffed through his mustache. "A homeless old woman might be out there in this storm. Got a flashlight with ya?"

Slate pulled a four-cell Maglite inside his parka and flipped it on. The light made a bright spot on the ceiling.

I squinted at the new brightness.

"See there." Slate flipped it off. "Keep one around all the time. Helps when I need to read a label in the back of a dark truck."

"Then tuck your pigtails in," Dalton told him. "Let's go for a walk."

"They're not pigtails. They're braids. Like a great Sioux warrior." Slate puffed his chest, and his braided hair swung from his face as he tossed his head.

—

"Not a damned thing." Dalton slipped in the kitchen door. Slate was behind him. Both stomped their boots and brushed layers of wet snow from their coats and the legs of their pants.

Dalton tugged the zipper down on his parka and pulled his cap from his head. He shook his shoulders and eyed Shelby, Claire, and me. "Nothin'. No sign of the plate. Just nothin'. It's damn cold out there, and that snow is blowin' hard. Filled in our tracks almost before we took the next step. I ain't saying she's not out there. I'm just sayin' we can't prove she is, or she isn't."

Slate pushed past us. He let his coat fall to the floor and turned his back to the oven with Shelby's cookies. "We tromped around the edge of the building as best we could," he added. "Wind chill's gotta be close to zero. You can't see more than fifteen-twenty feet in that wind and dark. I don't know what more we can do."

All of us moved to the windows. Shelby pulled Claire close. I could hear the waitress's soft sobs.

"Look there," Dalton said.

Not an arm's length from the glass, a half dozen elk, like black ink blots against the grays and whites, struggled through the deep snow.

"It's strange that they're so close," Shelby whispered as if anything louder would spook the animals.

Dalton shook his head. "It's this storm. Got the wind to their backs and walkin' with their heads down. Looking for someplace to hunker down and ride out the cold. Poor devils."

"I hope they find it." And I hoped Eva had found a warm place.

"Come on. All you. Help me with these cookies. The cook is

making coffee and cocoa." Shelby steered Claire away from the windows. "We'll build up the fire in the lobby. We've invited the guests. We'll laugh together. Tell stories. Maybe sing. And keep this old storm outside the windows where it belongs." And she touched the top of Claire's head with her cheek. "Ms. Randolph and the ladies are coming down. Doctor Kane said he'd bring Sugar. I think Miss Periwinkle will be there. Porsche and Odyssey, too."

Chapter 7

Steam rose from the mug Ms. Randolph handed to Tad Slate. The truck driver nodded his thanks.

"Dip the cookie into it." Nylon rustled on nylon, and she smiled at him.

Slate dunked the cookie. He licked the drops before they fell and then bit the cookie in half. "Umm. That's good. What is it?" He whispered and then leaned down.

"I had the bartender make it for me. It's hot buttered rum." She raised a finger to her lips. "Shh, I don't want everyone to know."

"It's real good." Slate sipped from the mug. "I heard about it but never had the pleasure. What's that I taste? It's something more than the rum. The spice, I mean."

"Nutmeg and cinnamon. I had to teach the bartender." She smiled at Slate again. "He wouldn't have known to add the spices if I hadn't have told him." Slate slipped his arm around her shoulders, and Ms. Randolph stepped away. "Would you like some, Mr. Hogan?"

I shook my head.

"Be careful, Tad," Ms. Randolph said. "It can sneak up on you if you're not careful. Especially at this altitude." She took three full mugs by the handles and balanced them in her small hands. There was a giggle in her voice. Carrying all three, she shuffled to the end of the couch closet to the fireplace, and held out the warm drinks.

Porsche untangled one mug from the others and took a sip. Ms. Randolph let Odyssey take the next mug, and she plopped down on the couch next to the artist. "Tell us about the fourth floor, Mr. Brown. You know about the families that stayed here and the spirits of the children," Ms. Randolph pleaded. "I love that part. And it is so important to Odyssey's work."

People on the other couches and chairs nodded approval. Popcorn was passed, and half-full trays of cookies made the third trip around. Dying flames in the fireplace lit shadowy smiles on faces.

When Doctor Kane reached down and tangled his fingers in Sugar's hair, she did not pull away. "More, Mister Brown," the doctor chuckled, "tell us about the fourth floor." He handed his longneck Coors to his wife, reached into his front pocket, and plucked folded bills from his money clip. He dropped the bills into Mr. Brown's hat at the edge of the fireplace.

Shelby nudged me. She'd traded her skirt and blouse for jeans and a thick turtleneck. "Brown never misses a chance to put his hand out for money. I saw him ask the bartender to break a ten. He fanned the bills, put them in his hat, and set the hat near the fireplace." She hid her smile with her hand. "Seed money, he called it. Stories for tips."

Brown was on his second cup of Ms. Randolph's rum. His back was toward the fireplace. Yellow and orange outlined his silhouette and hid all but his eyes in the twisting shadows.

"He tells a good story. And he looks the part, too."

Brown wore the same crumpled white shirt from earlier. His tie was undone, and as he gestured, the brass buttons on his blazer flashed in the firelight.

Shelby raised on her tiptoes and whispered in my ear. "I'm going to let this be his last story. We need to send these people to their rooms soon. And you and I promised to help Odyssey and Porsche set up the pictures."

"So, the auction is going to happen?"

Shelby shook her head. "Maybe the storm will break tonight, and a few more bidders might dare the weather and trickle in." She held up crossed fingers. "Porsche and Odyssey insist. Porsche already had several bids from those who saw the catalog. She thinks they have enough high-dollar bidders here. Besides, if we're stranded because of the storm, it will be good entertainment while we wait for the power and plows."

I glance at the lobby clock. It was twenty minutes to eleven. I took the last chocolate chip cookies and rested my hip on the edge of a table. "I think I want to hear this story. He said it was about children." I looked back at the restaurant door to see if little eyes were looking back. I bit the cookie in half and let the chocolate melt on my tongue.

Shelby plucked the half-cookie from my fingers and popped it into her mouth. Her eyes were brighter than the firelight. "This story is my favorite." She chomped the cookie. "I've heard it a dozen times, and I still like it."

—

Brown's hands were large. He pointed toward the Billiard Room, and from his fist, the shadow of a finger, twelve feet long, unrolled across the wall. "We talked tonight about the poor woman who fell to her death on the stairs behind those doors. Some nights, workers hear her last screams as life ebbed from her broken body. And I told you of the loyal hotel worker who was burned to death in a natural gas explosion in a guest room just above us." The tip of the shadow's finger pointed to the stairway. "Remember. Somehow the very next morning after the accident, friends found that she had reported for work. Or someone else had punched her time card at precisely five minutes to seven."

Brown took a sip of the rum. "And there is that unfortunate construction worker. Trapped when one of the tunnels collapsed. He called for help in the only way he could. The tap of his hammer on the stones that became his coffin. Many late nights, guests who dare to go downstairs hear the sound of that hammer still."

Brown tipped the bottom of the mug to the ceiling. His tongue searched for the last drops. He set the mug on the mantel and turned back to the dark room. "Those and others are the tormented souls. The ones who seek to escape. But there is another group of spirits that haunt these halls. Ones who have chosen this special place because of some precious memory."

Near the fireplace, Porsche leaned forward and tilted her head to hear more. Sugar Kane took her husband's hand and squeezed it. Ms. Randolph wrapped her arms around Odyssey. The artist rested her cheek on the woman's shoulder and leaned back on the couch. Her eyes were closed. From a solitary chair at the back, the orange dot of a cigarette glowed from Miss Periwinkle's lips. Around the dark lobby, others waited for Brown's next words.

"This grand hotel opened its doors in 1909. Remember, the world was much different then. It was common for a working man to have never left the county or even the city where he was born. Only the very rich could afford to travel. But the rich, yes, the rich. What is it they say about the rich?" Brown paused. It was a practiced pause. He had told this story before.

Shelby touched my hand. "Listen, Guy," she whispered.

Firelight showed Brown's smile. "The rich are very different from you and I. Travel was by trains in 1909. Besides the cost, one had to consider the time involved in traveling from, say, somewhere in the East to this refuge in the Rockies. Families would come for a month or more. Some spent the entire summer season. Men would hike and fish. Ladies sketched pictures of the wildflowers and took walks on the grounds. Nights were for dinners and concerts."

Brown raised a hand. "Did you know that John Philip Sousa was a frequent guest and performer? Dinner was always served on the finest china. Guests were expected to wear their very best. It was not uncommon in those days for a woman to travel with two dozen dresses in six trunks. Business deals were consummated on the porch with whiskey and cigars. But what about the children?"

Brown turned to the mantel. He found his mug, and he pointed. The question spread across his face. Shelby shook her head. Brown frowned and put the mug back.

"These privileged children were sent to the fourth floor." Brown let his audience absorb his words. "The families' nanny would accompany them. It was a wonderful vacation for them, also. Pony rides, a fishing pond, games, ice cream. Families would return year after year. Friendships grew. And for these little ones, the summers became a place of adventure. A place they would not forget.

"Later, as the gloom of world wars and the Great Depression swept over, the memories of those summers became a refuge. When death wrapped tight around them, some sought one more visit to this place of fresh air, mountains, and friends. On some late nights, if you listen, you can hear them laugh in the fourth-floor halls. Some of you might even be fortunate enough to see little eyes peek around corners in ghostly games of hide-and-seek. They come because of the good times they remember. One more visit before they pass on."

Brown stopped. Ears around the room listened for a child's laugh. I searched the door to the Cascade Room.

"Surely, you must have seen them, Odyssey?" Brown asked. "You painted their pictures so well."

Odyssey stiffened. She pulled away from Ms. Randolph. "What?" she blurted. "No." Her eyes widened, and everyone stared. "I mean, yes."

"Of course, you saw them." Above the murmurs, Ms. Randolph said, "Odyssey, of course you did." And she wrapped her arms tighter around the artist's shoulders.

—

Around the dark lobby, smiles left the faces. In a flare from a match, Miss Periwinkle lit her next cigarette. A haze of gray smoke lifted into the dark, and the woman shook her head. Sugar turned to look at her husband. Doctor Kane moved away from the couch and cocked his head.

Shelby stepped into the circle of firelight. She tugged the sleeves of her turtleneck up to her elbows and began to clap. "Let's thank Mr. Brown for his wonderful stories of this creepy old place." Others in the room joined in the applause.

Ms. Randolph pulled away from Odyssey and clapped the loudest. She turned to her friends on the couch, and they joined in.

Jim Hayes nodded his approval. "Good job, Brown," he said for all in the lobby to hear.

Shelby raised her arms. The crowd settled down. "My personal thanks, Mr. Brown. I still get shivers every time you tell those stories. Tonight was no exception."

Brown tipped his face forward in a polite gesture of thanks.

I thought he was enjoying the appreciation too much.

"I have a couple of announcements to make while we are all still together." Shelby rose onto her tiptoes. "First, the restaurant will open for breakfast tomorrow morning at seven. You know we're short on staff. So, our chef has decided to serve breakfast buffet style. He promised two kinds of eggs, bacon, sausage, ham, freshly baked sweet rolls, crepes, waffles, and fruits—I'm sure you will be able to find something you will enjoy. And because of the challenges this storm has presented, hotel management thought we should express our thanks for your kind understanding. The breakfast buffet is complimentary. Our way of saying thank you."

Everyone in the room again applauded.

"Next, you're all wondering about the auction. We're happy to tell you that things will go on as planned. If the storm moves on and they're able to plow, we're hoping more will join us."

Again, polite applause rose from the room.

Shelby smiled. "Finally." Her fingers found a strand of hair on her cheek and tucked it behind her ear. "I need each of you to retire to your rooms. The hotel needs to conserve fuel for its backup generators. We have no idea when the power will be restored. We'll need to dim the lights further in a few minutes." She shrugged. "When we dismiss from here, please be careful on the stairs. Sorry, no elevator tonight. If you didn't get one of the flashlights, we have a few more."

People began to gather their things.

Doctor Kane raised a hand. "Is the bar open for a nightcap?"

"I'm sorry, the bar is closed," Shelby said firmly. "But you're welcome to the last of the cookies as you head upstairs. And folks, it will be cold tonight. Housekeeping put extra blankets in all your rooms. Cuddle up and stay warm."

Doctor Kane took his young wife by the shoulders and squeezed. "You heard her, Sugar."

I moved across the room and found the wrought-iron poker beside the fireplace. I stirred the glowing coals and added two more pieces of split pine. The fire caught, and new light reached into the room. Guests paused at the front window to stare at the snow.

"It's still coming down," more than one muttered as they made their way to the stairs.

Some picked at the few remaining cookies and nodded thanks to Shelby. Ms. Randolph and her ladies gathered around Mr. Brown. He was smiling. Porsche and Odyssey stood by themselves near the door to the Piano Room.

I went to Shelby. "Nice way to shut things down," I told her. "And how did you get in touch with anyone in management to authorize the free breakfast?"

The stubborn bit of hair was on her cheek again. This time, she screwed up her lips and blew it away. "When they're not here, I am the management." Despite the long day, there was a sparkle in her eyes.

"They should sleep well."

"I hope so. The hot chocolate and Ms. Randolph's rum should help. And I made sure the coffee we served was decaf." Her freckles disappeared in the dark. "I should have added Benadryl."

Hayes joined us. "Sixty-seven," he said. "That's what registration counted. We may be off by one or two. And at least forty-some were here in the lobby. Good job keeping the natives from growing restless." He nodded to Shelby.

"So does that sixty-seven include us and the staff?"

"No, let me think. The three in-housekeeping. Claire, the chef, and his helper. That's three more. Liz and Jan at the front desk. You and Dalton. That makes ten. Shelby and I are twelve. Brown makes thirteen."

"Thirteen, huh?"

The pine wood in the fireplace snapped, and an orange ember arched into the room. Hayes smashed it under his shoe.

"Yeah, thirteen," he said.

—

"Mr. Brown?" I fumbled with a broken cookie. "Could I ask you something?"

Brown leaned his shoulder against the mantel. He had taken the tip money from his hat. He thumbed through the bills once and then again. A frown curled the corners of his mouth. He tucked the money into an inside pocket of his coat and lifted a mug from the mantel. "Ms. Randolph's only reward for my stories was the last of the hot rum. At least it's still warm." He squinted at me. "What do you need?"

"The spirits of the children? Do they stay on the fourth floor?"

Brown took a sip from his mug. "Oh, no. The staff insists that on some late nights, when they're alone at the front desk, the elevator will move. When they check, the elevator is empty, and they swear they hear children laughing." He raised his eyebrows. "The maids hear giggles while they're cleaning rooms. Doors shut when no one is there. Waste baskets are tipped over. The towels they have hung are on the floor. One desk clerk told me she saw a laughing child slide down the banister. But when she went to look, no one was there." Brown rubbed his eyes. "But most times, a guest reports little eyes watching them from behind a door."

Brown looked over my shoulder. The frown reappeared.

"What about the restaurant? Has anyone seen one of the children's ghosts near there?"

Brown set his empty mug on the mantel top and began to walk away. "Sounds like you've seen Betsy, Mr. Hogan. I'd like to hear all about it sometime. Now, if you'll excuse me." He brushed past me.

—

"Lower your voice." Porsche backed away from Mr. Brown.

"You promised." He took a step forward. "I did exactly what you asked. Now give me what you said you promised."

Porsche's next half-step pressed her back against the locked door of the Piano Room. She turned her face away from Brown. "The storm," she whimpered. "The storm has complicated things. You'll get your money, but you'll need to wait until after the auction. I promise."

I snapped up the poker from beside the fireplace and hurried across the empty lobby.

Brown's large hands hung at his sides. He turned and saw me, and his hands knotted into fists. "You said tonight," he hissed at Porsche. "That's what you said. I want it now."

Porsche cringed. "I don't have the cash. You'll get your money. I'm good for it."

"Can I help?" I thumped the sooty end of the poker on the floor next to Brown's foot.

Porsche let out a breath. From the corner of my eye, I saw Odyssey crouching, like a scolded child in a shadowy corner.

"I want it now," he snarled. "How do I know I can trust you?"

"What's going on?" I touched the end of the poker an inch from the toe of his shoe. For the first time, our eyes locked. Strings of spittle hung from his teeth, and I smelled the rum on his breath. I made my words slow and even. "What's. Going. On?"

Porsche touched my back. "There's been a bit of a misunderstanding."

Brown huffed a foul breath. I moved the end of the poker closer to his foot.

"I understand Mr. Brown's income was affected by Odyssey's event. I really do." Porsche stayed behind me. "I told him that if he would add some stories about the ghosts and spirits that"—she stepped forward a bit—"inspired Odyssey, it might help with the auction. Sort of marketing, you know. I promised him a nice gratuity."

"You said five hundred dollars," Brown spit back.

"Yes. Yes, that's what I said. And I intend to pay you. It's just with the storm and all, I simply forgot. I don't have the cash. When the hotel's office opens tomorrow, I'll get you the money."

Brown pumped his fists open, then closed. He started to raise a hand.

I tapped the poker on the floor. "Sounds to me like you'll have to wait until tomorrow, Mr. Brown." He stepped back until his face was lost in the dark. "I heard her promise. She means to pay you. You need to be patient. This storm has us all a bit uneasy."

The light from the dying fire cast dark shadows across the hollows of his cheeks. A snarl spread across Brown's lips. He paused like he was about to speak, then turned and walked away.

As if one of the spirits from his stories reached out a hand, a bit of paper fluttered from his coat. I reached down to pick it up. It was a twenty-dollar bill.

"Mr. Brown," I called out. "You dropped this."

The shadows seemed to sense where he would step. Darkness hid him as he walked back. His face was ghoulish, and he snapped the bill from my fingers. When he turned, he let the darkness swallow him.

Only when we heard his shoes on the stairs did Porsche take a breath.

"Thank you, Mr. Hogan. I don't know what I would have done if..." Porsche wouldn't look up at me. "Like you said, the storm has us all a bit uneasy."

—

Shelby pulled her hair into a loose ponytail. She crossed the lobby with Jim Hayes. In the shadows, her teeth sparkled from the smile on her face. Porsche stood with Odyssey, and both women looked out the window at the swirls of falling snow. The lobby clock chimed once, and old popcorn and cookie crumbs crunched under my boots.

Porsche left Odyssey at the window and met us at the door to the Piano Room. "Were you able to move the crates with Odyssey's works upstairs?"

Hayes nodded. "They were able to get everything on the dumbwaiter. It took three or four trips. They worked with flashlights and an old lantern one of the men found. Everything is in the Billiard Room, like you asked. There. It didn't take as long as I thought it would."

"Can I see?" Porsche tipped the top of her head toward the door. Not a hair fell out of place.

"Got your key, Shelby?" Hayes asked.

"Crap." She stamped her foot. "Excuse me. But I left the key in my other clothes." She shrugged. "How about I go upstairs and get it? I want to change out of this good sweater anyway. You might want to change, too." Shelby pointed at Porsche's calfskin boots and her tight cashmere. "Say, I'll meet you back here in thirty minutes. It will be just after midnight, like we planned."

Porsche nodded. "Good. I'll have Odyssey come with me." She walked to the window and touched the artist's shoulder. Porsche took a plastic flashlight from her handbag. It carved a yellowish shaft across the dark lobby, and the two followed it to the stairs.

Hayes whispered, "Those two aren't the easiest to work with. I'll bet they'll want more than just these flashlights to set up all those easels and pictures."

"We don't have anything but flashlights."

"I was thinking." Hayes turned to Shelby. "Remember that outdoor wedding we had here about a month ago? You used those old-fashioned kerosene lanterns? What happened to those?"

"They're in my office. But I'm afraid there's no fuel." She blew the stray hair off her cheek again.

"I think I know where maintenance keeps a five-gallon can of kerosene. It's downstairs. If we're lucky, there might be some fuel left. I'll get Dalton to go with me. Hogan, can you go get the lanterns from Shelby's office?"

Heat waves shimmered over the dying coals in the fireplace. The next gust rattled the windows, and the wind moaned.

"I'll go with you, Mr. Hogan." In the darkest corner of the lobby, Tad Slate's face appeared over the top of an overstuffed chair. The red glow from the fireplace turned his braids into twisting tentacles across the floor.

"Have you been sitting there this whole time?" Shelby glanced at me.

"Yes, ma'am. Just sittin' here enjoying the dark. I do that a lot." Slate turned on his Maglite. We squinted at the new brightness.

"Yeah," I told him, "I could use some help."

Shelby tangled her fingertips in my shirtsleeve. I turned to look at her. She pressed her office key into my hand. "Be careful," she mouthed.

I wanted to see her eyes. But her eyes were lost in the dark.

—

I followed Slate down the stairs to the hotel offices and the long hall where I had met Ms. Randolph, Brown, and the ladies with the ghost tour. It felt as if weeks had passed since I heard Odyssey's scream and felt the weight of the headless rabbit in my hands, but it had only been hours.

The beam from Slate's big flashlight glared off the walls, and over his shoulder, the bottom of the staircase seemed miles away.

"Hogan, you listen to all that stuff that Brown fella was talking about? Bad spirits and goody-goody ghosts?"

He didn't wait for my answer. "He sure plays it up, doesn't he? Standin' there in that dark suit with the fire at his back. Kinda gave me the shivers. And those big ole hands of his—ah—making weirdo shadows on the wall. Them ladies on the couch with that artist girl, they were scared. I was watchin' 'em." He paused before taking the next step. "What about you, Hogan? You believe in ghosts?"

I should have said, "Maybe," or "I'm not sure."

I would have been sure before Dalton parked his truck in the hotel's lot. Many of those who gathered around the fireplace to listen to Mr. Brown weave his strange tales believed. Some believed because the stories entertained. Others, I was sure, would swear the once-dead visited us. According to Brown, they were here to ease some unsettled torment or to spend more time in their favorite place.

What about the child at the restaurant door? Brown called her Betsy. She smiled at me. But she wasn't there.

I wanted to blame it on things I understood. I was tired. It was late. I had eaten. Everything I had heard about Odyssey's paintings and what Brown had told the ladies on the ghost tour planted little suggestions in my head.

The mind plays tricks.

Fatigue was to blame, I told myself.

Betsy. The little girl ghost had a name. And what about the headless rabbit?

If I were an honest man, I would tell Slate, "I don't know." Instead, I asked, "Do you believe?"

He said, "Hogan, you hear that?"

—

Tap.

Tap. Tap.

The sound was faint and far away.

Tap.

Tap. Tap.

All around us was quiet. The sounds of Slate's breathing fell in rhythm with the noise.

Tap.

Tap. Tap.

"It's that darn ghost. The one that's trapped and wants to get out." Slate hurried down the stairway.

The glow from his flashlight went with him, and darkness wrapped around me like soft velvet. The vibration of his steps shook the stairs. I tugged the plastic flashlight from my pocket. It slipped from my fingers and rattled down the stairway.

Tap.

Tap. Tap.

I drew in a breath. The air turned thick and warm. Everything in me told me to turn back and hurry to the lobby.

Tap.

Tap. Tap.

One at a time, the hairs on the back of my neck rose. What was I afraid of? There was an answer. The sound was of water in the boiler. Or a door rattling on its hinges. Perhaps warm air in the furnace ducts. The empty hall and cement floor magnified the sounds.

Tap.

Tap. Tap.

I sucked in the next breath and followed Slate. My flashlight rested on the second step from the bottom. I snatched it up. My thumb found the switch and pushed it forward—a pale, yellow beam blended with the garish light from Slate's Maglite.

Slate laughed. "Lookee this. I almost browned my drawers. See it, Hogan?" He pointed with his flashlight. "Right there in the corner."

It was a plate. Jenny would call it a dinner plate. Someone had pushed it into a corner. The wet cement all around it gleamed back at us.

Tap.

Tap. Tap.

"They got 'em a leak." Slate's flashlight followed the corner to where the ceiling and two walls met. Moisture turned the sheetrock brown. Paint peeled. Not six inches from the walls, the corner of a ceiling tile sagged. As if it were held there by some ghostly force, a drop of water clung to the saturated panel.

As I watched, the drop grew larger until it pulled free and fell.

Tap.

Another drop formed and fell. Then another.

Tap. Tap.

I pushed past Slate and shined my flashlight onto the plate. The bottom of the plate slanted toward the walls. Each drop fell onto the high side and puddled in the low. Not even a half an inch of water had accumulated.

"Wasn't a trapped ghost with a hammer, Mr. Hogan. Just dripping water and an old plate. That's all."

"Yeah," I said. "Let's find those lanterns and head upstairs."

I watched the next drop fall into the pan. The floor around

the plate was wet. If it had been there since Shelby and the others came upstairs, there would have been more water. Someone had set the pan there after the floor was wet. But why? And who knew we would find it?

Tap.

Tap. Tap.

Someone or something.

"Slate, you never answered me. Do you believe in ghosts?"

"Sure do."

I picked up the plate, spilled the water on the floor, and tucked it in the back of my jacket. I wanted to show it to Shelby. If I was right, it was like the plates that were used in the restaurant. My burger had come one just like it.

Tap.

Tap. Tap.

Chapter 8

The scent of kerosene wiped away the last smell of the popcorn and cookies. In the beam of a flashlight, Dalton held a funnel to one of Shelby's lanterns, and Hayes tipped a five-gallon can into the funnel.

"That's 'bout enough," Dalton said. "We filled the first two lanterns up all the way and divided what was left of the fuel between the other four." The old ranger unscrewed the stem from the base of the lantern and began to pump the shaft in and out. "This builds up air pressure in the fuel tank. When I open this valve—" He twisted a lever at the base of the glass—"the pressure sprays a mist on the silk mantle." Dalton set the lantern on the floor. He found a kitchen match in his vest pocket, struck the match with his thumbnail, and slipped the lighted end into the globe. The flame wrapped around the mantel, and the lantern glowed.

Dalton huffed out a deep breath. "Just somethin' about the light from a lantern late at night. It's so different from all the new battery stuff folks are using. Kerosene seems warm and quiet, not cool and angry like electric. Light from a lantern reminds you not to hurry." Dalton chuckled. "Maybe I was just born at the wrong time." He chewed on the ends of his mustache.

"Hogan, I'm gonna set one of the full lanterns on the front desk and leave the full one and the rest of the lanterns by the door to the Piano Room. That should give you enough light to set up the pictures. And if it's not..." He shrugged. "I need you and Hayes to head on up the stairs. He needs his rest, and I want you to get off your feet for a few minutes. Slate, you go with 'em."

"I was gonna sit down here in the dark for a while," the truck driver said. "I do that a lot."

"Not tonight, you ain't." Lantern light sparkled off Dalton's teeth.

Slate shook his head and pointed his Maglite at the stairway. Hayes stood, and the two followed the electric beam up the stairs.

"Get goin', Hogan." Dalton pointed for me to follow. "I'm goin' to check things out again. I'll wait here 'til Shelby and those two women get down here."

"Are you going to help us with the pictures?"

Dalton shook his head. "No. I volunteered you for that. I'm bettin' there's gonna be a whole lot of 'yes, ma'ams' while those pictures get hung. You're better at being polite than I am." Dalton slid my duffel across the floor with his foot. "Go on now. See you in a few minutes."

—

I opened the door to room four seventeen and tossed my gear on the bed. The air was icy cold. I used the flashlight to search the corners of the rooms for little eyes, and then I laughed at myself for looking.

Dalton told me to get off my feet for a few minutes. Instead, I paced to the window to check the snow, then crossed the room, rested both hands on the bathroom sink, and stared into the mirror. The faint light from the plastic flashlight cast yellowish shadows across my face. I looked old.

And I was.

Doubts swirled in my head like the snowflakes caught in the wind outside. The dripping water explained the sound. Was the plate from the restaurant? If it were, anyone could have taken one. But who had placed the plate there? How did they know we would find it?

I glanced at my watch. It was ten minutes to midnight. I couldn't wait. I wanted to see Odyssey's art. More than anything, I wanted to see the portrait of the ghost girl, Betsy.

I splashed cold water from the sink onto my face, toweled off, and shut the door behind me. Shadows darker than in my room filled the hallway. I listened for childish voices and watched the corners for little eyes.

Please prove you're really here or get out of my head.

I stopped at the top of the stairs and listened.

"Guy?" It was just more than a whisper. I recognized the voice. It wasn't childish. Or ghostly. It was Shelby.

She sat in the window seat at the end of the side hall. It was as if the shadows had painted her there. She pulled her legs up in front of her, wrapped her arms around her knees, and leaned her back against the wall. She patted the cushion beside her.

"Turn off your flashlight. Don't spoil it." Her breath made hazy clouds on the windowpanes.

I turned off the light, settled onto the seat, and turned to look outside.

"I never thought there could be so many shades of gray." She touched the glass with her fingernails. "No lights from the town or cars. Not even a sound, but us talking. It's the way it should be. I don't want to go downstairs. I just want to sit here forever." Then she laughed. "I'm sorry. I think I let you peek at my dreams."

"It was a nice dream. But we have work to do."

She tucked that strand of hair behind her ear. "A minute more?"

"Okay."

"Two minutes?" She smiled.

I shook my head. "Something's bothering you. You told me to look at Odyssey's neck. Why?"

"You spoiled all this, Hogan."

"I'm sorry, and I'm tired, and I want the lights to come on." I rubbed away the cloud my breath left on the window. "I want to know why I should look at that girl's neck. What am I supposed to see?"

"She's old."

"What?"

"Women can do things with their hair. They can paint on makeup. Wear the right clothes. Even pay a surgeon for a facelift. All that to look younger, but the neck always gives it away." Shelby raised her chin and touched her throat. "This morning, I saw these terrible wrinkles."

Her throat looked perfect to me.

"So, Odyssey's neck is old?"

"Not just her neck. She's old."

"So, she's older than she says. Big deal. Women lie about that all the time."

"Listen to me. Her bio says she worked here at the hotel ten years ago. She'd dropped out of college or something like that. You know, to find herself. So that makes her early twenties. Let's say twenty-two plus ten years is thirty-two. Her neck shouldn't look like that. She's petite and acts childish, but I swear I think she's closer to forty."

"So?" I tried to picture Odyssey in my mind. Images blurred. She was wrapped in a winter scarf when I saw her with the rabbit. I'd only seen her in the shadows tonight, with Porsche and on the couch while Brown told his stories. I hadn't looked at her neck. "Maybe she's older. What difference does it make? Maybe Porsche cooked that up to make her pictures more appealing. I don't know."

Shelby touched my leg. "Hogan, I'm not sure she ever worked here."

"What?"

"Listen to me. I asked around, and no one seemed to remember her." She paused. "Except Jim Hayes. He says he remembers her. He seems so sure of it. So, I did something else. There's a place at the top of the back stairs where, over the years, people have tacked up staff pictures."

I nodded. "Hayes showed me the pictures when he was explaining about the dumbwaiter and how they were going to bring the Odyssey's pictures to the Piano Room. I saw him in one of the pictures. But I never thought to look for Odyssey."

"I looked. Twice. I saw Hayes, Claire, Liz from the front desk, and others I recognized. She's not in any of the pictures. I'm sure."

"There must be some record of her employment. Did you check that?"

"I did. But it seems they changed the system three years ago, and all the old records are stored in banker boxes off-site."

"So, Odyssey and Porsche invented all this to make her pictures more..."

"Valuable," Shelby said. "Did you see the starting bids in the catalog?"

"Yeah." *Two hundred fifty thousand for Betsy.* "I can't believe how much those silly pictures are worth. If you're right, we're talking fraud."

"I don't want to be part." She shook her head. "It could hurt the hotel's reputation. Those ladies with Ms. Randolph. They might believe in something that isn't. What can we do?"

I sat for a moment and thought. "Let's do this. After we're done with the Odyssey and Porsche, we'll go back to the top of the stairs and take another look at the pictures. Maybe you missed her. Maybe we'll find her. If she's there in a picture, we'll know. How does that sound?"

I thought for a moment more. "Wait here. There's something I need to show you. I'll be right back."

"What is it?"

"Just wait. It's in my room."

I hurried down the dark hall, fumbled for my key, and dashed inside. I snatched the plate I had found downstairs and went back to Shelby.

"Look at this." I flipped on the flashlight and held out the plate. "When Slate and I went downstairs to get those lanterns, we heard something..." I explained about the sound, the dripping water, and where we found the plate.

Shelby took the plate from me. She turned over and tilted toward the light.

"That's the plate I found. Is it from the restaurant?"

"I'm sure it's one of ours. Anyone could have carried it off."

"It's just so many things don't fit together. Maybe I'm making more of this than I should. But for now, let's get downstairs. They'll be waiting for us."

Shelby stood up. "And Guy..."

Downstairs, the lobby clock struck its first tone.

"I know, look at Odyssey's neck."

Chapter 9

The twelfth stroke of the clock in the lobby faded away.

Shelby's fingertips grazed the back of my hand. "It's midnight," she said.

I thumbed the switch on my flashlight back and forth. There was no light. I smacked it on the palm of my hand, flipped the switch again, and a weak beam nudged at the gray shadows around us.

"Darn it."

Shelby held out her flashlight. "Here, use mine?"

"Let's save it. We might need yours later."

She slid off the window seat and followed me down the dark hallway.

From three floors below, the glow from the kerosene lanterns turned the shadows of the railings into twisting monsters that threatened with each creak of the old stairs. Dalton was wrong. Tonight, the light from these lanterns was angry, not at all quiet.

Porsche waited on the second-floor landing. "I heard you

coming." She took a deep breath and gazed into the dark all around us. "It feels so different without all the people."

When she lifted her face to look up the staircase, I raised my flashlight a bit so I could study her throat. Even in the dark, I found places along her jawline where the skin wrinkled like tissue. Shelby was right; a woman's neck told a story.

"Where's Odyssey?" Shelby asked Porsche.

"She couldn't wait to get started. She's already downstairs."

"By herself?" Shelby's eyebrows arched.

"Ms. Randolph's with her."

Shelby stiffened. "But I thought bidders weren't allowed to see the pictures until the viewing before the auction."

"That was what we planned. But Odyssey insisted." Porsche quickly added, "Odyssey's terribly fragile. Ms. Randolph seems to help her. We'd best hurry."

From the lanterns Dalton had placed on the fireplace hearth, a pale half-circle of light pooled in the lobby. Shadows of couches and chairs flowed across the floor. In the center of the lobby's largest window, the lantern light printed a bright star-shaped reflection. Beams spread from the star and touched every edge of the glass.

Another lantern sat on the table near the door of the Piano Room. From it, yellowish ripples blended with the light near the fireplace. Above the quiet, wind-driven snow danced on the moaning gusts.

I snatched up the lantern from the fireplace and followed the ladies to the Piano Room door.

Shelby called Odyssey and Ms. Randolph. "Ready to get to work?" She fished the Piano Room key from the back pocket of her jeans, slipped the key into the lock, and opened the door.

I lifted the lantern, the globe hissed, the light dimmed for an instant, and a breath of cool air touched my face. The room was dark. The shadow from the open lid of the grand piano spilled across the floor like an eerie liquid, and the lantern's light chased it away.

Shelby stepped back, and Ms. Randolph led the others into the room.

"This will be so perfect." Ms. Randolph babbled. "Odyssey child, have you thought about how you'd like to arrange your pictures?"

I stepped inside. The glow from the lantern warmed the room. Odyssey crossed to the piano and turned her back on the rest of us.

"Odyssey, child. We need to get to work. Where do you want your pictures so people will see them?" Ms. Randolph coaxed.

Odyssey shrank back into the dark. "I'm just not sure. I-I haven't thought about it."

Porsche moved to Odyssey. "Remember what we talked about?" She put an arm around the artist's shoulders. "Ms. Randoph, Odyssey has thirteen pictures. We talked about putting six easels along that wall." Porsche pointed to the wall that separated the Piano Room and Billiard Room.

Ms. Randolph nodded her approval. "Yes, and angle them so that each picture faces people coming in from the lobby."

"I like that," Odyssey whispered.

Porsche hugged the artist tighter. "We'll do the same with five more on this side of the piano."

"Okay." Odyssey stepped away from Porsche. "Is that all right?" she asked Ms. Randolph.

"I like it, child," the older woman answered.

"We'll save the place behind the piano for your newest piece." Odyssey looked at Ms. Randolph. "Do you like that?"

"Very much." A smile spread over Ms. Randolph's face.

"But it's so dark," Odyssey whispered. "I'm having trouble thinking."

Porsche looked at me. "Can we get more light in here? You said there were other lanterns."

I nodded. "Yes, ma'am." I handed the lantern to Shelby and went to the lobby door.

"What will you do with the last picture?" Shelby stepped

into the center of the room and raised the lantern. Light spread and glimmered on the piano keys.

"Right there. Where she's standing." Porsche said. "People can gather. Sip the champagne. Nibble on hors d'oeuvres. Chat."

"And decide how much they'll bid." Ms. Randolph beamed. "This will make you very rich, child."

"Which picture do you want to put there?" Porsche asked.

Ms. Randolph looked at Odyssey and whispered, "Betsy."

I jerked around to look at the women.

Odyssey smiled for the first time.

"You know the one with Betsy in the restaurant. Put it right there for your fans to see, child." Ms. Randolph took Odyssey's hands in hers. "It's one of your best. People will love it."

I hurried into the lobby to get the other lanterns.

—

"What's wrong with you, Hogan? You seen a ghost or somethin'?" Dalton struck a match and lit a lantern. New light crawled over his face. He sucked the drooping ends of his mustache into his mouth.

"I might have," I mumbled.

"Huh? What'd you say?"

"Nothing." I lit the last lantern.

"That's not what you said."

"Never mind. I'm just tired."

Dalton sat back on his heels and tipped up the brim of his Stetson. "I thought this job would be a stroll in the park. You and me was just gonna stand around all stern-faced and watch rich folk look at paintings." The old warden shook his head. "You was right, Hogan, we shoulda gone huntin'."

"Help me take the lanterns in."

"Nope. Told you I don't get along with women. That's why I sent you." Dalton struggled to his feet. "'Member to be polite."

"What are you going to do?"

Dalton dusted off the knees of his jeans. "Head on upstairs. See if I can get a couple of hours' sleep. As soon as you're done in there, you should do the same."

I nodded.

"Anything else?" he asked.

"Yeah. Dalton, do you believe in ghosts?"

He smoothed his mustache. "I've walked this earth long enough to know there are things out there no one can explain." He turned and walked off. "See you at breakfast, Hogan."

—

The light from the five lanterns brightened the room. Shelby set easels along the wall and put five more between the piano and the windows. Porsche and I opened the crates. Ms. Randolph showed each painting to Odyssey, and the two selected where it would be placed.

"Hogan, take a look." Shelby pointed at the first row of paintings. "Look familiar?"

"That's the elevator in the lobby, right?"

A man and a woman stood in the elevator. A bellman had wheeled a luggage cart of suitcases in next to them. A room key hung from the bellman's pocket. All the faces blurred in the dark so that I seemed to see these people only from the shoulders down. The bellman's hand pressed the button for the fourth floor. Subtle brushstrokes added a tiny pair of hands near the buttons. Those fingers pressed the buttons for the second and third floors.

Ms. Randolph moved beside us. "I can almost hear the little ghost giggle, can't you? Now the elevator will stop at every floor. Such a naughty little child."

"Look closely, Hogan," Shelby said. "See the number on the room key in his pocket. Four seventeen. Isn't that your room?"

"Yeah." I swallowed hard.

Ms. Randolph smiled. "Odyssey has a talent for doing things like that. She seems to sense who will see her pictures." She moved to the next easel and studied the art. "I'm trying to decide which ones I'll bid on."

It was easy to recognize the scenes from the hotel. There was nothing special about the artwork. The paintings seemed a bit crude. The backgrounds were something a child could paint, and some seemed unfinished. But in each, as if a different set of hands and brushes had added it, playful eyes or little fingers set for mischief challenged those who looked not to smile. Tiny fingers moved the pencil just out of reach of the woman at the registration desk. Other fingers moved the hands of the lobby clock back an hour. Little eyes watched a maid search her pockets for room keys, while the keys rested on the floor near the maid's bare feet.

Shelby and I moved from one easel to the next, and both of us smiled at the scenes we saw. "I was expecting something more frightening," Shelby whispered.

"Come," Porsche called as she set a painting on an easel near the grand piano. "You must see Betsy."

My guts clinched. I followed Shelby.

This picture was larger than the others. Porsche had placed it where the light from the lanterns was the best.

"Do you know about Betsy?" Ms. Randolph asked.

"Just what I've heard," Shelby answered. "Betsy is supposed to be a helper. That's what everyone says. As the maids finish up their cleaning, they find mints already on the pillows, and even the ends of the rolls of toilet paper in the bathrooms have been folded into neat triangles. Waitresses tell me when they're sent to dress the tables for dinner, the salt and pepper shakers are full, the napkins are folded, and the silverware is polished. They say, 'Betsy helped me.'"

"Have you ever seen her?" Ms. Randolph wiggled between us.

"No. I know workers who swear they have," Shelby said.

"I would like to see her," Ms. Randolph said. "What about you, Mr. Hogan?"

I couldn't answer. I stared at the picture. Like the others, the background was crude. But I recognized the door from the lobby into the restaurant. A man stood there. Again, his face and shoulders disappeared into the unfinished top third of the canvas. Instead of straight on, the view was from a lower corner and looking up. Perhaps what a six-year-old child would see. There were no little eyes or mischievous hands; instead, a little girl looked up at the man. It was the girl I had seen. Every detail I remembered was there. Even her smile.

All our eyes fell on one detail. Shelby gasped.

"Look, Mr. Hogan," Ms. Randolph said. "The man in the picture. He's wearing your boots."

—

I stepped back, but my eyes never left the picture. The little girl's head tilted. She was smiling. When I examined the smudge of paint under the windows at the back, two women sat at a table. Could they be Shelby and Porsche?

The painting's crude brushstrokes and the blur of colors made it seem like a dream. A dream from six hours earlier. How did the artist paint this picture from tonight, months ago?

I looked down at my feet and then at the picture. The man was wearing my boots.

From behind me, beams from flashlights slashed the darkness in the lobby like razor blades.

Jim Hayes's voice was first. "Stop. You can't go in there."

But a woman burst into the room. Like a knife thrust, a beam from her flashlight stabbed at Porsche's face.

"What is she doing here?" the woman raged.

I stepped up. But the woman pushed past me. She towered over Ms. Randolph. "How dare you?" She spat out the words and then turned back to Porsche. "This is unethical."

Hayes put his hand on the woman's shoulder. She shrugged it off.

"Do not touch me."

"Get out of here," Ms. Randolph hissed at the woman.

Hayes reached out. The woman rapped his knuckles with the plastic flashlight. "You will not touch me," the woman snapped.

"How dare you?" She turned to look at Porsche. "I should tell the others what's going on here. And I will right now."

Porsche stepped closer. "Delores, please."

"It's *Miss* Periwinkle. And do not patronize me. You swore that none of the bidders could see Odyssey's work until the viewing before the auction. What? The rules don't apply to *that* woman?" Miss Periwinkle jabbed the plastic flashlight at Ms. Randolph's face.

Ms. Randolph slapped it away.

"Ladies," Hayes shouted.

"This does not concern you." Delores Periwinkle sneered. She stared at Ms. Randolph.

Ms. Randolph set her jaw and stared back.

"Miss Periwinkle, please." Porsche tried again. "Odyssey asked for Ms. Randolph's help, that's all. You're right, I should have—"

"That's no excuse," the English woman said. "You have an obligation to us. You know I've attended shows like this all over the world. Never has the artist nor the event promoter done anything like this. It's a small industry. I intend to let everyone know. You violated a trust."

Porsche gathered her thoughts. "Do it," she said. "Run upstairs and bang on every door. Do it now. Tell your colleagues. Tell everyone." Porsche smiled. "Tell them that the pressure of a first show...and this storm. All of it. Trapped in the hotel. No electricity. Not knowing when it will end. Patrons canceling. It all weighs terribly on Odyssey. The world knows she's fragile. She sought out a friend. Tell them that."

Porsche raised a finger and pointed it at Miss Periwinkle's face. "And you decided this kind gesture somehow intrudes on you. Tell everyone how offended you are." She paused. Her hands dropped to her sides. "Now get out. Get out now, or I will have Mr. Hayes and Mr. Hogan help you leave." And she turned her back.

Silence draped the room as dark as the shadows.

Miss Periwinkle looked at me, then back at Porsche. Odyssey cowered in the darkest corner of the room.

Shelby broke the quiet. "Please, Miss Periwinkle. I think you should do as she asked."

Miss Periwinkle's eyes flamed. She said nothing but turned and walked out the door and into the dark lobby. The beam of her flashlight lit the stairs.

"I'll decide in the morning whether you will be allowed to attend the auction," Porsche called after her.

—

No one spoke.

We finished our tasks. Porsche placed a card on each painting with the work's title and the suggested opening bid amount. Ms. Randolph sat on the piano bench with Odyssey. Odyssey buried her face in her hands, and the older woman stroked her hair. Jim Hayes stood nearby.

I gathered the wrapping paper from the paintings and stuffed it into the crates. Shelby opened the door to the Billiard Room, and I placed the first of the empty crates along the wall of the Billiard Room and out of the way.

As I stepped through the door, the lantern near the piano sputtered, dimmed, and went out.

Odyssey's head snapped up. "What's happening?"

Ms. Randolph looked at me.

"It ran out of fuel. There wasn't enough to fill up all the lanterns," I told them.

Odyssey trembled. "Will the others go out?"

"I'm sure they will."

"How soon?" the artist whimpered. She raised her head and

turned to look around the room.

I moved closer and looked at Odyssey's throat. But the shadows hid her neck. "Soon. But we're almost finished," I told her.

"Can I go?" Odyssey looked at Ms. Randolph.

"Child, there's one more picture to put out. The one you just painted. You told me, it's your best."

"Not now. Please. I'm so tired."

Porsche tipped her head at the last picture. It was twice as large as the others. It was still wrapped in brown paper and rested against the wall beneath the window where Jim Hayes had watched me hide the headless rabbit.

I turned toward the door of the Billiard Room. Hayes had the keys to it. He'd unlocked the door when we came up from the back stairway. I remembered that afternoon when Shelby showed us the Piano Room, how she remarked that the door to the Billiard Room should have been locked. Thoughts turned over in my head. It was no mere chance he'd been at the window.

I studied the shadows in the Piano Room. Dampness showed in Odyssey's eyes. Ms. Randolph held her hand. Jim Hayes bent down and whispered in Ms. Randolph's ear.

"Jim," Shelby called out. "I think you should leave, too."

Porsche nodded. "She's right."

Hayes straightened. He started to speak, "Wh—?"

Shelby stepped into the center of the room. "Porsche asked Mr. Hogan and me to help with the setup. Odyssey invited Ms. Randolph. Given Miss Periwinkle's objections, it is probably best if the five of us finish things. You should rest. You'll have a lot to do in the morning."

A second lantern hissed. Its light faded away, hiding Hayes's face in a new shadow.

"Odyssey?" Hayes asked. "What do you think?"

The artist looked at Porsche first. Then at Ms. Randolph. The older lady nodded. Odyssey turned to Shelby.

The third lantern sputtered. Light faded, and the lantern went dark.

"Jim," I said. "Please. It's best."

Hayes shook his head and left the room without a word.

Porsche waited for a moment and then called to me. "Help me with this." Together, we placed Odyssey's last picture, still in its wrappings, on the easel near the room's side windows.

Something rose inside me. I wanted to tear the paper away and see what images the artist had conjured. Porsche stopped me.

"There," Porsche said, "we won't unwrap this one until the auction."

—

Shelby and I put the last empty crates in the Billiard Room. We listened for the others to leave. The clock in the lobby chimed.

"It seemed like that took more than an hour," I said.

"I know," she said. "Is it just me? Was that tense?" She crossed her arms and fought back a shiver. "I don't like the way I feel about this."

"Something else is going on here that I don't understand. Like how Hayes knew to follow Miss Periwinkle and why Odyssey seems to need Ms. Randolph's approval." I looked at my watch. It was just after one. "Let's walk over to the kitchen. We'll wait a few minutes until we're sure everyone's gone. Then let's go take a look at the pictures of the staff."

"Yeah, but there's something else I should have told you upstairs. You're not going to like it."

I took a deep breath.

Shelby flipped on her flashlight. The shadows from the empty crates pasted images that looked like gravestones on the wall. For an instant, the wind held its breath, and the new quiet slipped in around us.

"Remember when Porsche told us Ms. Randolph was a rich hotel heiress? That she could buy this hotel ten times over?"

I nodded. "I remember."

"Listen to me. I was at the front desk when she and those other women checked in. I took her credit card and got her a room key. About an hour later, Liz from registration called me. She told me Ms. Randolph's credit card was declined. It happens almost every day, so I wasn't alarmed. I told her to run again. But they had. Twice. Still, no go."

"Okay."

"I told them to have a bellman take a note to her room. Explain the situation and request another form of payment. It's what we do in those cases. I didn't want to do anything to embarrass her. Last night, before we got together in the lobby, Liz told me Ms. Randolph called the front desk with a new credit card number. The card was approved, but get this. The name on the card was James Hayes." She shrugged his shoulders to fight off the cold. "By then, the phones were down, and she couldn't call the credit card company to verify it."

The cold found me. Goosebumps rose along the center of my back.

"What should we do?" Shelby's eyes pleaded.

I shook my head. "What can we do? Maybe it's best to wait. As soon as we get the phones back, have Liz call and double-check with the credit card company. James Hayes is a common enough name. Like you said, it happens all the time. It might be nothing."

"I wish the lights would come back on."

"So do I," I whispered. "So do I."

Chapter 10

Shelby shut the Piano Room door. She rattled the key in the lock, tugged on the doorknob, and then looked up at me. "Tell me I'm being silly, but there's two million dollars' worth of painting in there."

"No, you're not." I reached out and tried to turn the doorknob. "It's best to double-check. And"—I snatched the top of a straight-back chair and slid it in front of the door—"You've got the only key, right?"

Shelby nodded.

"You're sure?"

She nodded.

I glanced at the chair I'd moved. "I'm the one being silly. Dalton said he thought something was off-kilter. He said he could feel it. I don't know what it is, but maybe he's right. Now c'mon."

Spilled popcorn crunched under our feet. Glowing orange threads in the fireplace ashes made the only light. Outside, the storm pounded the windows. We wove our way around the lobby couches and chairs. Shelby turned on her flashlight and pointed the beam at the restaurant door, where I thought I'd seen Betsy. I hesitated for half a second.

Shelby touched my shirtsleeve. It was what Jenny used to do in quiet moments. Right then, Shelby reminded me of my Jenny, but not all.

"Let's wait here. We don't need to go to the kitchen."

The hiss from the kerosene lanterns on the landings above was the only sound. Light drifted down the stairs in waves and seemed to dissolve as it touched the cool air from the lobby.

Strength ebbed out of me. I was tired. My mind was confused. I thought about sleep and wondered if an off-kilter world would ever allow it.

Above us, a door slammed shut. Flashlight beams slashed the gray shadows along the staircase. Another door creaked as it opened.

"Did you hear that?" a hoarse voice whispered from above.

Shelby hurried up the stairs toward the voice.

"We heard it, too," the second voice answered.

"I was almost asleep when I heard it. It sounded like it was right outside my door."

I caught up with Shelby on the third floor. Ms. Randolph stood in the center of the dark hallway. Her spiky hair was wrapped in a white turban. A floral robe fell to her knees. Beneath it, her cotton nightgown brushed the floor, and she wore thick gray socks. "I know I heard something." She craned her neck and pointed her flashlight down the hall.

"Heard what? What did you hear?" Shelby was breathing hard from the climb.

"We heard it, too." Doc Kane stepped into the hall. Tufts of white hair showed on his bare chest. He wore shiny satin pajama bottoms, and his cowboy hat sat perched on his head. Sugar leaned on the doorframe. She tugged at the hem of a Texas Longhorns T-shirt. The shirt barely reached the top of her thighs, and she stepped back when she saw me.

"What did you hear?" Shelby demanded.

Doc Kane looked at Ms. Randolph.

"It sounded like—" Ms. Randolph paused.

"A little girl was laughing." It was Sugar. "More like giggling. Really."

Doc Kane tipped back his hat. "She's right." He cleared his throat. "It was a child. Giggling. Like Sugar said. It sounded like she was right here." He tilted his head toward the hall between their open door and Ms. Randolph's room.

The world's kilter shifted again. I searched the shadows for Betsy.

"There's nothing here," Shelby said. "Are you sure? Could it have been the wind?"

All three shook their heads. Then Doc Kane spoke. "I've been a pediatrician for more than thirty years. I know what a child's laugh sounds like."

I stepped in. "A building this old can groan and creak. Especially with this storm and all this wind. Maybe—"

Doc Kane's eyes flared. He raised his voice. "I know what I heard."

From down the hall, the door to the room across the hall from the Kanes opened a crack. A flashlight inside painted a bright spot on the floor. In the spot of light something moved across the carpet from the room into the hallway.

Ms. Randolph gasped. Sugar shrank back into her room.

"Corey, no." It was a woman's voice.

I trained my flashlight on the thing on the floor. It was a car. A child's toy.

The door opened wider. A woman looked into the hall. The little boy from the restaurant—the one with the hamburger, he'd fallen asleep at the table—stood with his mother.

"I'm so sorry. Corey was so keyed up from those ghost stories downstairs." She patted his shoulder. "He refuses to go to sleep. He wanted to play with his new toy. I tried to keep him quiet. We didn't disturb you, did we?"

Shelby smiled. "Not at all. I think those stories have us all..."

Doc Kane took off his hat and covered his bare chest with it. He smiled. "I feel a bit foolish."

Ms. Randolph sighed. "I think I'll try to sleep. See you all in the morning." And she shut the door to her room behind her.

"I am sorry," Corey's mother said. "I hope we didn't—"

"Don't worry," Shelby told her. "Everything's fine."

Corey pulled away from his mother and reached down for his toy.

"That's quite a car you got there." I hunkered down on my heels so I could see the boy's face.

He snatched up his toy. "It's not a car, Mister." His face grew stern. "It's a Gobot." His little hands twisted the toy. In the shadows cast by my flashlight, what had appeared to be a little car became a robot. Tiny tires turned to reaching arms, and instead of a steering wheel and a windshield, a menacing face stared up at me.

"It's not what it seems," Corey told me.

—

It's not what it seems.

Maybe the kid, Corey, was more right than he knew.

Things weren't what they seemed.

A kid's toy car wasn't a ghost haunting the hallways. Water dripping wasn't a trapped soul's hammer. Odyssey's paintings, this dark hotel, and Brown's stories had stirred everyone's imagination. Including mine.

Shelby's concerns about whether Odyssey was who she claimed to be were more important now. Was this whole thing a fraud and a plot? Perhaps there was a clue we needed in those snapshots of the employees on the Billiard Room back stairs.

I told myself not to think about Betsy.

And the ghost child was all I could think of.

I had no natural explanation for her. Was she the power of suggestion? I told myself no. Fatigue. It had to be fatigue. I was just tired.

I nodded to Shelby. We slipped away and kept to the shadows as we climbed the steps to the lobby.

Shelby tugged on my shirtsleeve. I turned to her. "Guy?"

"I heard it, too."

I put a finger to my lips. "Shh."

The floor of the old hotel moaned under our feet. The hinges on the massive front door squeaked. Outside, gusts of wind brushed the windows. Each insignificant sound battered the quiet.

Shelby's lungs drew her first breath in minutes.

I shook my head. *Had my imagination again created something that wasn't there?*

But Shelby heard it first.

I let out a breath, not wanting that bit of noise to mask the sound I waited for. I dared not inhale.

"It sounded like a woman," Shelby whispered. "You heard it, didn't you?"

I nodded and touched my lips again.

We waited.

Warm air rushed through the heat vents. Gears in the works of the lobby clock turned, and the minute hand moved one click. Curtains rustled. A blackened log in the fireplace snapped as the dying fire cooled.

With each faint click of the clock, minutes passed. Soft sounds filled the silence. But the sound we wanted never came.

"Wait here," I whispered to Shelby.

"No."

"I'm going to get a lantern from the other room."

"I'll go with you."

"You scared?"

"Yes."

"I think I am, too." It seemed so funny.

She caught her laugh in her fingers. "Maybe I didn't hear what I thought I did. It was just my imagination."

I couldn't answer. I let the quiet take over.

Finally, "C'mon, let's get a lantern."

"Then what?"

"The pictures. I need to see those pictures of the staff."

—

I lifted the lantern and held it close to my ear. Fuel sloshed in its tank. "Not quite half full," I told Shelby. "It should last long enough for what we need to do."

"Just look at the pictures, right? Nothing more."

"Yeah."

"Promise?"

"I promise." I didn't want to add unless we heard the sound again.

I unscrewed the plunger on the lantern's side and pumped air into the fuel tank. When I released the valve, the fuel mixture hissed on the silk mantle. I slipped a lighted match into the globe, and pale light bathed the lobby.

Though I forbade it, every new shadow became a ghoul.

Shelby gasped. She saw it too. Then, "This is silly." Shelby shook her head. "Shadows turned to goblins. Old buildings make noises. We've been on our feet all day. Neither of us slept since last night, that's all."

I held up the lantern. She followed me through the Piano Room, and we headed for the Billiard Room. But, still, the shadows from the art on the easels clung to the walls like giant, hungry spiders.

I needed to chase away the strange and find a bit of normal to grab onto.

"Tell me about yourself," I asked her.

"What?"

"The job here? How did you find it? Or did it find you?"

"Now? You want to talk about that now?"

"Yeah. I want to forget about fraud and ghosts. And noises in the dark. I don't want to worry if there's enough fuel in this lantern. Whatever normal is, I want it to be normal for a few minutes."

Even in the shadowy dark, I watched her shoulder relax. She let out a deep breath. "I think I do, too. Normal. Whatever that is. I need it too."

I sensed her smile. The one I remembered from when her face wasn't hidden in the dark.

"Where do you want me to start?"

"Wherever you'd like."

"How about a farm town in Nebraska? It's home, and it's all I ever knew. Family farm. Fourth generation."

We stepped into the barroom that separated the Piano Room from the Billiard Room. This time, the shadows on the wall from the crates were only boxes, not gravestones in a moonlit cemetery.

"Your father was a farmer?" I coaxed.

"A good one. He worked hard. He complained about grain prices, too much rain or not enough, and the price of diesel. And gas. And fertilizer. He drank coffee with men just like him at the café in town. The only times I saw him without a John Deere hat on his head was at the dinner table or church. We went every Sunday. He was nearly bald, and his forehead was as white as a ghost." Then she laughed.

I did too. Then, to make her tell me more, "What about your mother?"

"She worked harder and never complained. I have two younger sisters. I complained about them and everything else."

"And?" I pushed the lantern in front of us, and we followed its light into the Billiard Room. Now, the billiard tables were only tables, not hulking four-legged giants waiting for us in the dark.

"My calf won a red ribbon at the county fair when I was fourteen. I was a cheerleader when I was a sophomore. Like I was supposed to, I fell in love with the star quarterback. He was a senior and was drafted when he graduated and went away. I wrote to him every day. We were married on the Saturday after my high school graduation. That's what everyone thought we should do. The whole town came to the wedding. He shipped out to Vietnam two weeks later." She paused. "He didn't come back."

"I'm sorry."

"No, he wasn't killed. But he was different. Maybe it was what he saw or did over there that changed him. Or maybe he wasn't what I wanted him to be. Or maybe I never really knew him. How could high school kids know? Anyway, I got a good job at the bank." Pain slithered into her voice.

I should have told her to stop, but she went on, like it had been inside her for too long.

"He wouldn't work. Every night, he'd go to the only bar in town. I didn't, and one day he put a pistol to his head. I thought it was my fault, and so did the whole town."

"You don't have to—"

"God, I haven't talked about this in years." She took the lantern from my hand and led the way. The floor creaked. The draft moved the heavy curtains. "Maybe my ghosts will keep the other ghosts away."

She told me about her life. "I left town the next month and enrolled at the University of Nebraska in the big city of Lincoln. My boss at the bank sent a letter to a banker he knew, who hired me, and I took night classes and threw myself into my studies. The next year, two women I met at school and I started a business. Just a small store. Women's clothes. I wanted nothing to do with farms. I poured every minute into that store. It became my whole life. We did well. We opened another store in Omaha. Two stores became four. Then six."

We stopped outside the door to the landing with the pictures we came to see. But she needed to tell me more, and I needed to listen.

"By then, my partners had husbands and kids. So, I bought them out. Paid the loan off in three years. Eight years later, I was going to their kids' graduations and weddings, and all I had was six stores. I sold to a competitor. I was going to travel. Made it as far as here. These beautiful mountains are so different from a Nebraska farm. I bought a little place. I was going to fix it up. That lasted two months. I got bored and applied for a job here. Now I work just as hard as when I had six stores. Maybe I need a job to keep my ghosts far away." She shrugged her shoulders.

The lantern hissed, and I reached for the door.

"You didn't tell me about you."

"I live alone with a beagle named Zac."

"I think I'd like to meet Zac." She found my face in the glow of the lantern. "And Guy, Dalton told me about your wife. You must have loved her very much."

I remembered another woman. She used those same words when men with guns stalked us on a dark mountainside.

I turned the doorknob. "Let's look at these pictures."

Normal stayed outside the door.

—

Frigid air funneled up the narrow stairway from the loading dock on the first level. Beams from the lantern threaded into the darkness.

Shelby grabbed the railing with both hands and peered down into the dumbwaiter shaft. "This is where that woman fell. The one from Brown's story." She shivered in the cold.

"Careful. Don't stand too close."

But she didn't move. "Brown said it was the middle of the night. The man's wife was chasing her. She reached the steep stairs and grabbed the railing. The woman who was chasing her heard her fall. She didn't call for help. She stood right here and listened to the woman die."

The next gust of wind rattled the windows in the Billiard Room. The walls shook. Air as cold as outside streamed from the bottom of the stairs. The sound was faint. The chains that held the dumbwaiter moved with the wind, each link touching the next in an eerie tone.

She shrank back. "Was that what we heard?"

"Maybe." Goosebumps prickled my skin. "Or, like you said, maybe it was what we wanted to hear." I took her arm and led her away from the edge. "Odyssey worked for the hotel ten years ago?" I turned her so that the lantern light fell on the wall with the pictures.

Shelby looked at the pictures. "The bio Porsche put out for the event said ten years."

Bright-colored thumbtacks held each snapshot to the wall. The oldest pictures were black and white. Others were in color. In the glare from the lantern, the edges rose and fell with wind gusts from the stairs.

"See if you spot any with Jim Hayes. That will give us some idea of the year. You take that half." I pointed to the left, away from the stairs. "I'll take these."

Most were pictures taken at the end of the tourist season picnics Hayes had told me about. Staff members were dressed in shorts and jeans. They sat at picnic tables. Some played badminton or pitched horseshoes. Hot dogs and burgers filled plates. There were watermelons. Fists held Coors cans.

I skipped the black and white and studied the color pictures. I guessed those would have been taken sometime in the seventies.

"Look for the group pictures," Shelby whispered. "It's easier than trying to look at each snapshot. If she worked here, she'd be in one of the group shots."

"If she went to the picnic."

"We have to start somewhere." Shelby pulled up her collar against the cold.

"Here." I tapped a photo. "There's Hayes. In the back row."

We both looked. Hayes had more hair and less paunch. But none of the women around him looked like Odyssey.

"That's him here." Shelby pointed to another picture. We studied the faces.

"No, I don't see her," I said.

Shelby scanned her half. I looked over my photos. I found another group shot with Hayes in the center of the front row. But no Odyssey. In another picture, the group sat around a picnic table. Hayes's legs dangled from the tabletop. Others sat on the benches. There was a beer in his hand and the empty ones all around him, but none of the women were Odyssey.

Then I saw it. I moved the lantern closer. The picture wasn't a group shot. Men pitched horseshoes. Hayes was off to one side. He reached down and wrapped his arms around a woman's shoulders. Both of them were looking at the camera.

"Shelby, look at this." I plucked a picture from the wall and held it in the light from the lantern. "See her." I tapped the picture. "There with Hayes."

Shelby looked at the photo. She cocked her head. Questions spread across her face. She looked up at me.

"We were looking for the wrong woman."

Wind rattled every window as if the storm wanted to break into the hotel. The chains of the dumbwaiter clattered. The sound was clear, faint, and came from the bottom of the stairs. Shelby heard it too. It was a woman's voice. It came from that blackness at the bottom of the stairs.

"Help me."

—

Shelby tucked the snapshot from the wall into the front of her sweater.

"Shh." I grabbed the lantern and held it over the stairs. The passage was steep and narrow. The lantern's glow fought to show only the first few steps. Further down, inky black swallowed the light.

Cold air swept up the staircase in bursts, like the panting of something alive.

"Help me."

The words were clearer.

The sound didn't come from the tangled chains. It wasn't the wind. Or something our frightened minds conjured.

It was a voice.

"Help me."

And the voice added one more word.

"Please."

The next breath of cold air wrapped around my face. Chills shot down my spine. The lantern hissed. Fuel and flame battled to stay lit. I pulled it away from the current of cold air and snatched the plastic flashlight from my back pocket. When I thumbed the switch, there was no light. I smacked the light against my thigh.

Nothing.

"Please help me."

"Give me your flashlight," I told Shelby.

She pushed past me and aimed her cheap flashlight down the stairs. I craned to see the bottom, but darkness snatched away the weak beam.

"Someone needs us," Shelby wrestled past me. "I'm going down there."

I grabbed her arm.

She pulled it away.

"Listen to me. We'll leave the lantern at the top of the stairs, away from the breeze so it won't blow out. I'll go first. You stay close and shine your flashlight over my shoulder so I can see. Okay?"

She nodded. "We need to hurry."

I put the lantern on the floor, took a deep breath, and turned my head as I took the first step. "When Hayes showed me these stairs, he told me there were twenty-one steps. Count as you go." I remembered how dark it had been when I climbed the stairs with Hayes. "It'll be so dark that you can feel the black crawl over skin. Count the steps, or you won't know where you are. We'll go slow."

Shelby swallowed hard. She pointed the flashlight over my

shoulder. "I'm ready."

I ducked down. My shoulders brushed the wall on my left and the dumbwaiter shaft on my right. In two more steps, my body blocked the light from her flashlight. Thick darkness seeped in from every side.

"Help. Please help." Clear, but weaker.

My foot reached down, and the toe of my boot found the next step. We were nine steps from the top. Nine out of twenty-one.

Who was there? Was this a trick to trap us?

Step twelve. It was colder as if in one more second, ice would form on my skin, and my lungs would freeze. Shelby's fingers tangled in my shirt's collar, and her touch was icier still.

The stairs groaned under our weight. Three more steps.

Fifteen. Only six more.

"Please, please. I'm so cold."

Who was there?

My empty stomach knotted. Cold air scorched my mouth and throat. If it wasn't for Shelby, I would turn and climb away from the voice and hide by the dying fire in the lobby. The dying warm fire.

One more step.

"Help." Then only sobs.

Shelby pushed me. "Hurry."

I pushed back. "No."

"Eva," she shouted. The darkness swallowed her words.

Somehow, on the narrow stairs, she slipped by me. Her flashlight filled the darkness. The floor was wet and slick. Crooked fingers of snow stretched over the cement, redrawing themselves in every gust of wind.

"Eva," Shelby shouted again.

I stumbled down the last two steps.

"Help." Weaker still.

The beam from Shelby's flashlight found her. The old woman huddled in the corner. One hand found the chains from the dumbwaiter, and she tried to stand, but her legs failed. Melting snow puddled where she sat.

Her eyes and cheeks were hidden in the shadows, but her mouth moved. *"Betsy?"*

Shelby kneeled. She reached out and touched the woman's face. "No, Eva. It's me, Shelby. Claire's friend."

The woman's head tilted. *"Betsy helped me. She brought me here and went to find you."*

Shelby wrapped her arms around the woman. Both began to cry. Shelby turned. "Guy." Her eyes widened.

It was in the hallway to the loading dock. Where it had been only black, a match head flared. In that speck of light, tiny hands touched the flame to a candle.

A child giggled.

Tiny feet brushed the floor, and a tiny hand reached from the shadows and motioned for us.

"What is it?"

"She wants us to follow." Shelby struggled to her knees. She bent close to the old woman's face. "Eva, we need to go. Guy will help you."

I was there. Beside Shelby. I lifted Eva into my arms. She weighed no more than dandelion fluff. Her filthy, wet hair clung to her face. I was dreaming. But I wasn't.

"Thank you," the old woman whispered, "Betsy told me you would come."

Her clothes were soaked. The wet moved through my shirtsleeves and vest. I felt her chills and shivers. Warmth ebbed from my skin onto hers.

The candle flame was a speck in the cold night. It floated away, and we followed. Shelby's flashlight carved our way, and I held the old woman in my arms. In the room where we unloaded the pictures, snow funneled from the space at the bottom of the overhead door where Slate's truck rested.

The speck of light led us to the stairway that employees use to climb to the lobby. The flame bounced up the stairs like a child dancing away from us.

Then it went black.

We climbed the last few steps in the beam from Shelby's flashlight. At the top, candlelight flickered behind a half-shut door. Shelby reached for the knob.

"What's this room?"

"It's a place where the night clerks can rest." She told me. "There's a bed for..." And she swung the door open.

Wax puddled at the base of the candle in the center of a side table. The small bed filled all but a place to walk. The blankets were turned down.

I gently laid Eva on the bed. The Shelby was beside us. She smoothed Eva's hair.

"Thank you, Betsy," the old woman whispered.

The wetness of her clothes chilled me. A wisp of smoke from the candle found my nose. Outside the little room, a child's laugh teased the shadows.

—

If it was a dream, it was over.

The laughter was gone.

Normal had deserted us.

Running feet pounded the lobby's hardwood floor. Hinges on the hotel's great front door screamed. A man grunted with effort. Cold winds whipped in. I caught the door to Eva's room before it slammed shut.

I dodged around the end of the front desk. A metal flashlight clattered across the smooth stone entryway. I grabbed the front door and fought to keep the wind from slamming it shut. Against the swirling snow, the flashlight beam found the figure of a man. He was struggling through the snow. Long braided hair trailed from his head.

"Slate," I yelled.

He didn't stop, and in the next instant, the black and snow swallowed him up.

I called again, "Slate." But the wind stole the words before they left my mouth.

I snatched up the flashlight and aimed it into the dark. It bored a weak channel through wind-driven snow. I swung the light one way and then the other. In the glare, twirling snow reflected, and beyond that, only darkness. Cold seized my damp shirt, and my lips trembled.

I fought the wind to close the door, and pressed my back against the rough wood, trying to gather in what had just happened. Across the lobby, the door to the Piano Room hung open. A flashlight beam cut through the dark inside.

I hurried to the doorway. Jim Hayes held the flashlight. He kneeled in the side doorway of the Billiard Room. Where we had just been, a woman's figure sprawled on the floor in front of him. My flashlight found his face. He raised a hand to shade his eyes.

Words were barely formed in his mouth. "He killed her."

Chapter 11

H E. *KILLED. HER.*
Muscles stiffened. Joints refused to bend.
All my mind could see was the dark smudge on the floor.
I wanted her to move.
She wasn't dead. *No one had killed her.*
Her head and shoulders hid in the shadows from the door.
In a moment, she would sit up. I knew it.
"*Watch your head.*" I didn't want her to hurt herself. "*Look at me. No one killed you. You're sleeping. Yes, you fell asleep. It's late. We're all so tired.*"
She lay on her side.
People sleep on their sides. Should I shake her? Or touch her shoulder?
Long hair covered her face. Her knees bent like she was running. One shoe was missing.
I'll find it. It's here somewhere in the dark.
I dared not touch her.
You're fine. No one killed you. It's not—

Murder?
Murder?
Murder.
"Get help," I barked at Hayes.
I was on my knees. My back was against the wall. My fingers touched her throat. I pressed down.
What am I supposed to feel?
Her skin was still warm. But nothing.
I moved my fingers to her jawline. Still nothing.
I know my hands are cold.
I rolled her onto her back and leaned close to her face.
Was she breathing?
I COULDN'T TELL.
That first aid class.
Seven years ago? Was it that long?
Chest compressions. One hand on the other. Center of her chest.
I felt the line of her bra.
I'm so sorry. Forgive me.
Push down. Again. Push.
Again.
Again.
For thirty seconds. Then…
Two breaths.
I pinched her nose closed. My mouth covered her lips.
They were so cold.
I blew my air into her.
Wake up. Wake up, please.
Jim Hayes snatched up the metal flashlight I had dropped. He scrambled for the lobby.
It's so dark. We were alone. *Just me and her.*
I emptied my lungs into her again
Her chest. Find the spot. Press down. Again. Press. Again.
I mashed my eyes shut.
Jenny would pray.

Jenny would pray.
Jenny would...

—

The beam from a flashlight found the doorway. Another flashlight joined the first, and then there were voices.

I pushed down on the woman's chest again and again.

Don't give up.

Then, a new woman's hands covered mine. They were soft. She pushed me away. Her hands took my place. She pressed down on the woman's chest, found a rhythm, and continued what I had tried. I rolled away and sprawled on the floor. On my side, legs drawn up like I was running from something.

I tried. I tried. Please save her.

A man pushed past me and kneeled near the woman's face and head. His fingers searched a place below her ear. He bent down and put his ear near her mouth. After several seconds, he bowed his head. "Sugar," I heard him say, "you can stop now."

Flashlights were all around me. Shadows from legs. And arms. Heads. Painted over the walls. Outside, snowflakes made bright from the reflected light, swirled in the howl of the wind.

All was so quiet. Except for the pounding of my pulse and the rhythmic, sickening crunch of the compressions on the woman's chest.

"Sugar, it's no use." His voice was firmer. "Sugar, you can stop. She's gone."

—

"Everybody outta here." It was Dalton. "Now. Doc Kane, you and your wife hang back a minute. The rest of you out. Now." Without a sound, the people did what he asked.

He kneeled by me. "You okay, Hogan?"

I nodded. "Is she..."

Dalton sat back on his boot heels. His shirt was unbuttoned.

He looked up at Doctor Kane and Sugar. "Is she?"

Kane wrapped his arm around his wife's shoulders. Sugar buried her face in his chest. He nodded. "There's nothing anyone can do. No pulse. No sign of breathing. I'm afraid she's gone."

"Go on outside. Wait in the lobby. I might have more to ask after I talk with Hogan," Dalton told them. "Shut the door behind you."

Darkness coiled in the corners of the room and slithered to the edges of the beam from Dalton's flashlight to stare coldly at the woman's body.

I tried to sit. Dalton helped me.

"Okay, Hogan, what happened?"

"She wasn't breathing. I tried…"

"No, before that. Whaddya see when you got here?"

"Slate. He dropped his flashlight and ran out the front door."

"Did you see 'em drop the flashlight?"

I thought. "No. It was on the floor by the front door. I guess I thought it was his. He was running."

"Slate? You sure it was Slate?"

I nodded. "I'm sure. I saw his braids."

"See his face?"

I shook my head. "No."

Dalton's eyes searched my face. "I don't need to know what you thought you saw or what you assumed. Just tell me what you saw for sure. A woman's dead, Hogan."

"Yeah, yeah. I understand." *But where do I start?* "Shelby and I, we heard a noise and went down the back stairs. By the dumbwaiter. The noise. It was that homeless woman. Eva. You know. The one you and Slate went out to look for in the storm? Somehow, she got into the hotel. She was all wet and cold."

Dalton sucked on the ends of his mustache. "Nothing is ever simple with you, is it, Hogan?" He spat the words out. "Where's Shelby and the old woman now?"

"There's a room with a bed behind the front desk. Shelby said it's for the night clerks." I left out anything about candles and Betsy. "That's where we were when…"

"When what?"

"The wind. I felt it. Or heard it. It was from the front door opening. I—ah—I went out. The flashlight was on the floor. The man with braids was outside in the snow. Running away. I lost him in the storm." I looked at Dalton so I wouldn't have to look at the dead woman. "Where's the flashlight now?"

"Must be the one Hayes's usin'."

"Yeah, Hayes." I went on. "I shut the front door. There was a light in the Piano Room. I went to the door and saw Hayes kneeling by…" I tipped my head at the body on the floor. "Hayes said, 'He killed her.'"

Dalton rubbed his face with his hand. "We need to talk with Hayes."

"Yeah." I shook my head. "But Dalton, who was it that—you know—that helped me?" I glanced into the shadows because I didn't dare look at the dead woman.

"Hayes ran upstairs and was pounding on every door he could find. Shoutin' about a woman had been attacked. I heard the commotion and pulled on my boots, then grabbed my shirt. Old Doc Kane took off down the stairs. That little wife of his beat him down here. She's an ER room nurse. And a good one, I'm bettin'. It was them. They knew what to do."

I shook my head. "Should we get a blanket? You know to cover her." My stomach turned over.

"This is a crime scene. We ain't touching nothing. No tellin' how long 'til the sheriff gets here. For now, we need to keep folks out of here and keep our ears open."

"Who's out there?" I lifted my chin toward the door to the lobby.

"Doc Kane and Sugar. Hayes. The English woman. The little artist gal. Creepy old Brown. That Randolph woman. Her ladies. Just about everybody." He sucked on his mustache. "Everybody but Slate."

Chapter 12

Dalton helped me stand. He swept the room with his big flashlight. "You and Shelby were the last to leave that gathering in the lobby, right?"

"That's right." I stretched the truth. I didn't want to tell him about the staff pictures. Not now. "We came in here to double-check things before the auction tomorrow. Shelby thought she heard a noise from downstairs."

A wind gust rattled the windows, and the shadows in the room turned darker. Dalton flashed the beam into the Piano Room. "One of you lock the door?"

"Shelby had the key." I thought for a moment. "I don't remember."

"So, it could have been unlocked?"

"Maybe." I shook my head. "So, if it was unlocked. Maybe she"—I nodded at the body on the floor"—came back to check on something, and Slate or whoever snuck up on her?"

"But why kill her?"

We stood for a long moment.

I tried first. "Maybe it was the other way around. Remember how Slate was always prowling around in the dark? Say, he was down here. Saw the open door and came in. She"—I couldn't say her name. Not yet.—"caught him in here. And..."

Dalton made a sucking noise with his mouth. "Still, why kill her? She might have told him to leave. Say he didn't want to go? What was so important to kill for?" He swept his light around the room one more time. "Let me think this through. You set the pictures on the easels?"

"I unboxed the pictures. Shelby set up the easels where they wanted them. Porsche and Odyssey picked the place for each picture. Ms. Randolph helped."

"That old biddy was here?"

"Odyssey wanted her."

Dalton clucked his tongue. He moved the flashlight from picture to picture. "Hogan, why is that picture still covered?" He pointed through the door. "The one against the wall, behind the piano."

"It's Odyssey's last painting. No one is to see it until the auction. From the way they talked, they're counting on it to bring big money."

Dalton followed me into the Piano Room. I walked around the end of the piano to the picture. "Dalton, shine your light right here." I pointed. "Here at the corner." I leaned closer, careful to keep my shadow off the wrapping. "It wasn't this way last night. The paper's torn. Like somebody started to unwrap it." I reached out.

"Don't touch it."

I pulled back. "What's under there might be the reason she was killed. Don't you think we should—"

"No. Leave it for the sheriff. But right now, I think we should have a word with Hayes. And then that little artist gal."

"Dalton, there's one more thing I should tell you."

He shined the light in my face. "Now what, Hogan?"

I let out a breath. "Shelby. She thinks Odyssey might not be who she says she is." And I told him about Hayes's name on the credit card and the snapshots of the hotel employees.

When I finished, Dalton sucked both ends of his mustache into his mouth and began to chew. "Where's that picture of Hays and this somebody?"

"Shelby has it."

—

I couldn't look at the body again. Dalton shut the side door to the Billiard Room and left the woman in the cool darkness. It seemed so sad.

We pulled the door to the Piano Room shut behind us and twisted the knob to be sure the door was locked. Flashlights made spots on the ceiling. Others cast yellow ovals across the floor. Doctor Kane stood from the couch near the blackened fireplace.

"Is there anything we can do?" he asked. Sugar reached up and took his hand.

Dalton shook his head. "We need to get in touch with the sheriff and coroner. Has anybody tried the phones?"

Jim Hayes spoke up. "I tried. Still nothing."

"That's what I was afraid of." Dalton raised his voice. "It's three thirty, folks. It won't be light 'til six or six-thirty. The best thing is for all of you to go to your rooms. Try to get some sleep. I know it won't be easy, but try." He looked around the room.

Miss Periwinkle twirled the ends of the sash that knotted her long bathrobe at her waist. The woman was barefoot. Ms. Randolph's hair was tied up in a silly turban. She wore the top of one of her nylon jogging suits and the bottom of another.

From the yellow slivers of the dying flashlights, it seemed every face looked at me. They wanted me to say the right thing. To make sense of what none of us understood.

I wanted that too

An oversized gray T-shirt with a Texas Longhorns logo hung over Sugar's shoulders and breasts. Her hair was mussed, and she'd pulled on a tight pair of Levi's before she hurried downstairs. Her eyes were wet, and her husband's hand was on her shoulder.

Brown shifted from foot to foot. He wore an undershirt, trousers from his uniform, and stocking feet. His big toe found a hole in his sock. Absentmindedly, he picked at the hair on his bare shoulder. He stared at the storm outside the windows.

Hayes wore his blazer, white shirt, slacks, shoes, and socks. Only his tie was missing.

"Go on now," Dalton said to everyone. "Hogan and me will watch things down here. Try to get some rest. Please, folks."

"Lock your doors." Hayes stepped into the center of the room. "Lock your doors. A murderer is running loose."

"We don't know that," I blurted out.

Hayes drew up to his full height and faced me. He spread his arms and pointed at the Piano Room. "I surprised Slate in that room. He was kneeling over—ah—her. He ran out the front door when he saw me. What more do you need?" Shadows hid his eyes. His mouth was ghoulish. "And do you know something else? Slate might be back in here now. None of us is safe."

Windows rattled from the wind. Ashes stirred in the fireplace, and the sooty smell of scorched wood drifted through the lobby. Ms. Randolph reached for Odyssey. She dug into a pocket, came out with a Kleenex, and gave it to the artist. Both women sobbed.

Doc Kane spoke up. "Most of you don't know me. I'm a pediatrician from Houston. I practiced for thirty-some years. About the woman in there. We don't know what killed her." People turned to look at him. "By the time I got there, she had no pulse and no signs of breathing. Without extraordinary means, there was nothing else to do. Hogan did his best. The woman is dead. That's all we know for sure. Without a proper autopsy, we won't know the cause of death. It could be natural causes, like a heart attack or a stroke. Maybe it was an accident. She tripped on something in the dark, fell, and hit her head.

There's no way anyone can know. Authorities will demand a complete autopsy, I'm sure. Dalton is right. All we can do is go to our rooms and wait until morning."

"And pray that the storm breaks," I whispered.

Doc Kane took Sugar's hand, and the two walked to the stairs. Brown followed. Others stood from their places. No one spoke.

Hayes shouted, "And lock your doors."

Dalton huffed out a breath. "Go on, folks. Try to get some rest."

People shuffled past. Some glanced at the door to where the dead woman still lay. Most looked at the floor.

"Hayes? Could you and Odyssey stay for a minute? Dalton and I need to go over a few things."

—

Dalton added some split pine to the fireplace. He found the poker and stirred the coals. A thread of orange brightened with the breath of fresh oxygen. Dalton leaned close and blew. The coals glowed brighter, and in an instant, tiny flames jumped to the new wood.

I settled onto the couch.

Dalton sat back on his heels. Firelight spread across the floor and chased the shadows deeper into the room's corners. He tipped his head toward the couch. "Take a seat, Hayes."

Hayes bristled. "I'll stand."

"Fine," Dalton told him, "I'll sit." He hung his hip on the arm of the couch. He smoothed his white hair. "Hogan told me he was in there, helping set up the pictures for the auction. He said the dead woman asked you to leave, and that you weren't too happy about that. Any of that right?"

Hayes stepped back. The dark hid his face. "We were all on edge from the storm. You don't think I came back and killed her? That's ridiculous. What right do you think you have to even ask?"

"Just trying to understand what happened, that's all." Dalton shot a glance at me, then back at Hayes. "Mr. Hayes, I spent the last thirty-plus years in law enforcement for this state, seventeen of those in this county. You know I was a game warden. I investigated poaching, trespassing, and every sort of game and fish violation you can name. They called me in on unattended deaths—lost hikers, drownings, accidental gun fatalities. I'm on a first-name basis with the county sheriff. The deputy coroner and me went fishin' together two weeks ago. When this storm breaks, and it will, who do you think they'll ask first what happened here, me or you?"

Hayes edged back further into the dark.

Dalton said nothing. He strummed his fingers on the couch back.

I counted Hayes's breaths.

Finally, Hayes spoke. "Yeah, she asked me to leave. It was because—. That doesn't matter. I was in my room. Couldn't sleep. Too much on my mind. You know I'm responsible for these people." The floor creaked under his weight. "I came back down here. The door was open. Saw the light from the flashlights. I started across the lobby, got to the door, and saw Slate kneeling over her. He saw me and ran for it. Then Hogan showed up. A half-minute difference and Hogan would have been the first one. That's what happened. All of it."

I thought through what he said. Everything matched what I remembered. Except, I saw Slate bolt out the front door, and when I got to the Piano Room, Hayes was inside the room. He was kneeling over the woman.

"No reason not to believe you," Dalton told him. "If you think of anything else, let me know."

"Can I go?"

"Yeah, try to get some rest."

"Like that's gonna happen." Hayes edged back out of the shadows. Light from the fire flickered over his face.

We watched him walk up the stairs.

"I didn't know you knew the sheriff that well," I whispered. "First name, huh?"

"Yup. But when he says my name, it's always 'Dalton, you son of a bitch.'" He grinned. "And the deputy coroner is a woman. She don't fish. Know something else?"

"Hayes's holding something back."

"I think so, too."

"Hogan, go get Odyssey. Let's see what she says."

—

I added more wood to the fire.

"Odyssey." I motioned for her to come and pointed at the couch.

They were at the foot of the stairs. Ms. Randolph leaned closer to Odyssey's ear and whispered. The older woman touched the artist's face and tilted her head toward the half-circle of pale-yellow light from the fireplace. "Go on, child," she said.

Odyssey hesitated. Ms. Randolph touched her shoulder, turned, and walked up the stairs.

Dalton was still perched on the couch's arm. Odyssey watched her feet as she picked her way around the other furniture in the dark lobby. She crushed a crumpled Kleenex in one hand, nodded at Dalton, and sat at the far end of the couch.

"Can I get you something to drink? Water?" I asked her. "Or I might be able to find the last of the coffee. It won't be too warm—"

"It's Porsche, isn't it?"

The wind roared, and the chimney belched smoke. My eyes turned gritty with the smolder.

Dalton rubbed his hands together. "I'm afraid so."

"Why won't anyone say her name?" Odyssey touched her eyes with the Kleenex. "You all just say the dead woman. Say, Porsche. That's her name. She's not just a body or some dead thing." Then the tears came.

Her shoulders shook. Sobs racked up from somewhere deep.

I reached out to touch her shoulder.

She pulled away. She lifted her face to see Dalton. The tissue touched her eye. She dabbed a wet place on her cheek and wiped away another tear before it reached her jaw.

Light from the flames swept over her throat. From the introduction in the auction catalog, Porsche explained how a nineteen-year-old had worked in housekeeping for the old hotel. Ten years later, the pictures she painted from her memories became the eerie subjects of the now sought-after artwork.

The neck I saw wasn't a twenty-nine-year-old's or even a mid-thirties. Her earlobes sagged. The skin along her jawline wrinkled like crepe paper. Lines creased her jowls. It was what Shelby had wanted me to see.

Odyssey lowered her chin. She supped in a breath and wiped the tissue over her eyes.

"Can you think of anyone who would have a reason to hurt Porsche?" Dalton asked.

She shook her head.

"You know I need to ask this," Dalton said. "What about your relationship with Porsche? Everything okay?"

"Porsche was my best friend."

"We're talking a lot of money. Money can make people do desperate things?"

She shook her head and mopped the tears.

"Okay, last thing. Where did you go after you all finished setting up the room for the auction?"

"To my room. Ms. Randolph was with me. Ask her."

We sat there. No one talked. The fire crackled. Wind moaned.

She sobbed. "I need to go to my room."

"Go on," I told her.

I leaned closer to Dalton. "Something's wrong," I explained

what Shelby said about a woman's neck. "She's not twenty-nine or thirty. There's something she's not telling us."

Dalton looked at me and whispered, "Snot."

"What?"

"I arrested all kinds of liars. Fishing without a license, shot one too many pheasants, havin' a creel full on a catch-and-release only stream. Women are the worst. Some of 'em start bludderin'. Beggin' me to give 'em another chance. Rivers of tears flow. One thing I figured out. You can fake tears, but you can't make your nose run." He sucked the end of his mustache into his mouth. "That gal never once wiped her nose, Hogan. There's something she's not sayin' all right. Snot don't lie."

Chapter 13

Dalton followed me to the registration desk.

"I'll be back." Dalton tipped his head toward the stairs.

From the gap around the door, a candle flickered near the bed where Eva rested. Shelby leaned on the doorframe. She crossed her arms. Static crackled in the dry air, and the light from my flashlight painted her shadow ten feet tall. I wanted to see her face. She stayed in the dark.

"I was listening," she said.

"Then you know?"

"Porsche?" Her arms squeezed tighter around her.

"Yeah." I wanted to say more, but the words refused.

"Was she—" Shelby stopped herself. "Do you know how?"

"Did you hear what Doc Kane said?"

She nodded. "But my imagination keeps creating these terrible images. Blood?"

I moved closer. She dropped her arms and reached out with one hand. I took it with both of mine. She was icy. I wanted to pull her closer. I couldn't.

"There wasn't any blood. She was just on the floor. She wasn't breathing. I tried—"

Quiet wrapped around us like shadows. The lobby clock clicked off seconds that became a minute. Then two.

She spoke first. "Like that silly CLUE game. Porsche. In the Billiard Room. With a—" She couldn't finish. She mashed her eyes shut and shook her head as if the motion would chase away everything bad. "Where's Dalton?"

"He went upstairs to get his gun."

She shuddered. "Will you get yours?"

"He wants me to."

"Will that help Porsche?"

There was no answer, so I willed warmth into her cold fingers. "Eva?"

"She's sleeping. But, Guy, there's something else." She pulled her hand away, and my fingers went cold. "When I helped her out of her wet clothes. I hadn't seen it before, but there was a nightgown on the pillow. Just a plain cotton thing. But someone had left it there. Like they knew we'd bring her there."

"Did you hear anything more?"

"You mean like a little girl laughing?" She shook her head. "No."

"More candles?"

"Just the one she left in the room."

"She?"

"Betsy. You think it was Betsy, don't you? You think a child's ghost made the sounds so we would find Eva. Then the ghost led us to that room. Put a candle there. Turned down the blankets and left a nightgown. That's what you think? Tell me it is."

Raw wind pounded the hotel's front windows. Frozen snowflakes scraped the glass like sandpaper. Icy air squeezed through the gaps around the front door and through the building's every unsealed crack.

"We need to hang on 'til morning. It will be better, then."

"You don't know that." Shelby shivered with each breath of the freezing air.

The beam from Dalton's big flashlight swept down the stairs. We heard his footsteps. He paused at the bottom. He shined the light into the lobby and held it for a second longer on the door to the Piano Room.

"Everything good down here?" he asked.

"How could it be?" Shelby whispered.

"Yeah, I know," Dalton answered. "Hogan, go on, get your gun."

"Do I need it?"

"What do you think?"

"I locked it in the safe in my room. I think I'll leave it there."

"It's up to you." He rubbed his hands together, then lifted them to his face and blew onto his fingers. "Tell me 'bout this picture you found with Hayes and this woman."

Shelby fumbled with the front of her sweater. She reached inside and laid the snapshot on the counter. As if an invisible finger pushed it, the next gust of wind moved it toward Dalton. He pinned down the image with his thumb and trained his flashlight on the grainy details.

"Right there." I pointed. "Look closer and imagine the woman is ten or fifteen years younger than right now. Add a few pounds. See what we see?"

Dalton bent over the picture. He squinted and seemed to gather in every detail. He looked up. "This don't make sense."

"But you see what I told you?"

He shook his head. "I'd bet my pension on it."

I sucked in a deep breath. The next gust of wind lifted the corners of the picture. The front door's hinges strained.

Shelby breathed out what none of us would say. "That's Jim Hayes with his arm around a younger Ms. Randolph. It's her, isn't it?"

—

Dalton walked to the hotel's front window. "When's this storm going to break?" he asked no one.

A gust slapped the glass. "Damn wind," he muttered. He pinched the skin at the top of his nose as if he could squeeze away the picture he had just seen and the body in the next room. "I'm sure somebody out there is doin' their best to plow the highways and main roads. No tellin' when they'll get to us." Dalton turned to us. "All we can do is wait."

"We have to do more," I told him. "What if it wasn't Slate?"

"Hayes saw him."

"Can we trust Hayes?" I turned to Shelby. "Tell him about the credit card."

Shelby filled him in about the James Hayes name on the credit card in Ms. Randolph's room. "I thought it might be a coincidence. James Hayes is a common name. But not now, with this." She held up the staff picture with a younger Jim Hayes and a younger, slimmer Ms. Randolph.

"And," I added, "after folks were heading upstairs after the storytelling, I overheard Brown and Porsche talking. He wasn't happy. He had her up against the wall. I went over to see what was going on and to try to calm things down. Brown seemed to think Porsche had promised him some money. He wanted it right then. She didn't deny it. She told him she couldn't pay him until after the auction. He didn't like that but finally backed off. I'm not sure what would have happened if I weren't there."

"Money for what?"

I shook my head. "Not sure."

"Miss Periwinkle," Shelby said.

"What about her?"

"You weren't there, Dalton. She was incensed that Ms. Randolph was with Odyssey when we were setting up the pictures for the auction. She threatened to tell the other dealer. Called it unethical. I've never seen a woman so angry."

"So, what do we do?"

"I want to take a close look at her body."

"Hogan, no."

"Just look. Was she strangled or hit on the head? There's got to be a clue of some kind. If we know that, maybe we can figure out who killed her."

"You heard Doc Kane. We got no way of knowing if she was killed. Maybe she just died, Hogan."

"I need to look."

"Un-huh, no way I'm not lettin' you go back in there. You're not gonna go touchin' the body. I told you, we need to leave it for the sheriff and coroner."

"Maybe I'll see something. Come with me." I reached out. "Shelby, give me the key."

She fumbled in the back pocket of her jeans and came out with the key. "I'm going, too."

"Un-huh." Dalton tipped his chin at the room where Eva slept. "You got to stay with her. I'll go with Hogan. But all we're gonna do is look. Hear me?"

I nodded and swallowed hard. "Let's go."

Dalton scooped the key from the counter. He pointed his big flashlight at the lobby.

I pulled the hotel's plastic flashlight from my back pocket and thumbed the switch. The light failed. I hit the light across the palm of my hand, hoping to bring it to life. Nothing.

"Take this one." Shelby held out her flashlight.

From the bed in the next room, Eva moaned.

"No." I shook my head. "You might need it."

Candle flames in Eva's room twitched in the next breath of air. Shelby touched my hand. "Be careful."

Dalton waited at the Billiard Room door. He swung it open, stepped back, and handed me his flashlight. The crates and boxes cast their eerie shadows. The air, cold as a tomb, made each shadow flow like syrup. We tiptoed through the room, and I went to the side door.

I dropped to my knees and let the beam of Dalton's flashlight sweep over the floor. I dared not look at her yet. Marks from when I'd balanced on my knees when I tried to pump life back into Porsche marred the carpet. I could see where I had sprawled after Sugar Kane pushed me away and took over the useless task.

Everything faded into the gloom of black and countless shades of gray. I touched the patterns in the carpet, afraid they might be damp with blood.

But the carpet was dry.

Dalton kneeled behind me. His breath brushed my face. My pulse thumped in my temples. "Go ahead," he whispered.

Porsche rested on her back. Her arms were at her sides. First, I pointed the flashlight at her feet. One shoe was missing. I fought the urge to shine the light around the room to look for the missing shoe. Instead, I moved the light slowly up her legs to her waist and chest.

Her sweater bunched below her breasts, and I could feel again the crunching bones and tearing cartilage coursing through my hands. The light caught the links of a fine gold chain across the bloodless skin on her collarbone. Her hair covered her face except for one filmy eye that stared at me.

I bit back the bitter taste at the back of my throat and focused on her neck. I followed the gold chain to a cross-shaped pendant. Where the two bars met, a diamond shone back at me, electric bright. Her skin had lost its color. It was waxy. If I stared longer, I was afraid her skin would disappear and I would see each vein, muscle, and bone. Just below her ear, at the point of her jaw, the pale skin darkened. I wanted to touch the place. It was purple and oval-shaped.

I let out a deep breath and focused the light on the other side of her throat. Dalton saw it too. He leaned closer. Porsche's hair had seemed so full and vibrant, but now it hung from her face like blades of grass. Even her ears seemed to shrivel like autumn leaves.

There were three bruises. They were violet and tinged with crimson. The one nearest her jaw was the longest, and I could see where each finger had squeezed. The bruise on the front of her throat was angry and purple.

"God damn it," Dalton whispered. "Bastard snapped her neck."

Dalton grabbed the edge of the piano and pulled himself from the floor. I glanced back at Porsche's neck, and my mind filed away every mark and bruise. I handed Dalton his flashlight before I memorized more.

The old game warden shook his head. "We know Slate liked to prowl around in the dark. He finds Porsche in here. Maybe he came on to her? She'd have none of it. He gets a hold of her. The last thing she saw was his eyes."

The chill started at the soles of my feet, climbed my legs, and settled in the pit of my stomach. Hairs on my neck stood on end. My mouth went dry, and my lips trembled.

"You're just guessing."

"Hayes said he saw him kneeling over her. You saw him run out the front door. It had to be Slate. I had a bad feelin' about that man since he showed up here."

"But what about Brown? Or Periwinkle. Or even Jim Hayes?"

"Aw, hell, Hogan."

Chapter 14

I tipped my head toward the room where Eva slept. "How's she doing?"

"She's sound asleep. I don't think she's moved since you laid her in the bed." Shelby rubbed her arms to chase away the cold. "What do we do next?"

"Wait." Dalton huffed out a breath. He leaned over the counter and rolled his flashlight back and forth. "We're back where we started. We have to wait for the storm to break. Wait for the law to get here, however long it takes. Share all your suspicions with them. Show them that picture. What else can we do?"

"So, we just leave her body there. Pretend nothing happened?" I reached out and stopped the flashlight.

"What else? Go out in the snow, and track Slate down and drag him back in here. Beat it out of him. Huh, Hogan?" Dalton leaned forward and covered my hand with his. "Or maybe walk up to Brown and ask him real polite-like if he killed Porsche? Show that picture to Hayes and accuse him of running some scam?"

The wind rattled the front door. He pulled the flashlight from my grip. "Hogan, I've sat beside dead bodies all night waitin' for the law to show up. It's no fun. But it's what you do. We'll keep our ears up and wait. Hear me?"

I nodded.

Dalton raised his voice. "I said, hear me."

"Yeah, I hear you."

"Okay, then." He tapped the flashlight on the counter one more time and turned to Shelby. "What time will the chef start gettin' breakfast together?"

She squinted at her watch. "Anytime now. I promised I'd help him."

"What about her?" He tipped his head toward the room where Eva slept.

Shelby thought for a minute. "I'll go upstairs and get Claire and Liz. We'll need Claire in the kitchen. Liz can sit with her. She knows Eva."

Shelby glanced at me and then down at the floor. She turned on her plastic flashlight and went up the stairs.

"I'm serious, Hogan." Dalton switched off his flashlight and turned to me. His face hid in the greenish hue of an exit sign.

"So, what are we going to do?"

"The best we can, Hogan. The best we can."

—

Shelby's voice floated from the dark stairway. "Jim, you startled me."

"Can't sleep." We heard him say. "I'm going downstairs to check the furnace and generator. I've got to do something. I just can't sit in my room." And he plodded down the staircase.

Hayes's flashlight swept the floor. He paused when he saw Dalton and me. "Couldn't sleep," he told us.

Dalton groused, "We heard ya." He pointed at the stairs.

Hayes rubbed his eyes. He paused and tipped his chin at the

flicker of candlelight from the room where Eva slept. "Someone in there?"

"Hogan and Shelby found that homeless woman. She was hidin' downstairs." Dalton said nothing about the staff pictures. "Eva—That her name? She's sleeping."

"How did she get in here?"

"Not sure," I told him. "We think she came in through the dock door. Where the truck is stuck."

"She okay?"

I nodded. "Cold and wet. A bit confused. She's resting now. We'll ask Doc Kane to have a look at her later."

A draft funneled in from the cracks around the front door. I pulled up my collar. Hayes rubbed his hands.

"I'm going downstairs to check on the furnace and make sure the generator's got fuel."

"I'll come with you." I looked at Dalton. He cocked his head, and I followed Jim Hayes to the stairway.

—

Hayes wedged the flashlight between his side and one arm and rubbed his hands together. Steam from his breath floated through the light beam and disappeared into the dark above our heads. He fished a ring of keys from his coat's pocket, found the one he wanted, and unlocked a door. A hint of warmth touched my face, and a steady hum teased my ears.

"Generators still running." Hayes stepped into the little room. I lost him in the dark, and his flashlight played over the side of the machine. Metal clanked on metal. A whiff of diesel hung in the air. "About half a tank left. That'll get us through the day. I think we've got about enough fuel for one more night. I'll fill it up at suppertime."

He reached into the dark corner of the little space.

"Tell me something?" I asked. "Odyssey?"

"What about her?"

The beam of his flashlight disappeared behind the

generator. I watched his shadow bend down. When he straightened, he held the end of a length of pipe or metal rod on the floor. He leaned on it as if it were a cane.

"Did you know her when she worked here?"

He cupped his free hand to his ear. "What was that? Hard to hear over the noise."

I raised my voice and asked the question again.

"Yeah," he shouted, and he tapped the pipe on the floor. "She worked for housekeeping. I was a bellman then. She kept to herself. I didn't see her much."

"Did she live in the workers' building?"

"I don't recall," he hollered.

Hayes turned his back. He raised the pipe and smacked it on a round piece of ductwork that connected the generator to the outside wall. He hit the duct again. Metal on metal reverberated over the hum of the generator.

The clang hurt my ears, and I stepped back. "Whacha doing?"

He swung again. The noise was sharper. The sound stabbed so deeply that even the fillings in my teeth vibrated.

I shouted back. "What are you doing?"

He pointed the pipe at the duct. "Fresh air intake for the generator. Can't let it get clogged with snow. Hitting hard breaks up any ice." He turned sideways and slipped around the generator. The pipe was still in hand. He raised the flashlight and shone it in my eyes. I lifted my hand against the glare.

"Why all the questions, Hogan?" His eyes were just slits. He licked his lips. Light from the flashlight sparkled on his teeth, and strings of saliva stretched from his lips.

I moved half a step back. "I was talking with Claire last night," I lied. "She said she doesn't remember Odyssey at all. She's worked here almost as long as you."

"So?" The pipe tapped the floor.

I sucked my bottom lip over my teeth and bit down. A message for me spread across his face. The clank of the pipe on the concrete floor added emphasis.

"Remember, Hogan. Her name was Audrey then. She changed it to Odyssey. Maybe that's why Claire doesn't remember her."

"Yeah, maybe." I held his stare.

Seconds stretched. He tapped the pipe on the floor and lowered the flashlight to his side. Dark wrapped around us.

Finally, he spoke. "Let's check that dock door. Maybe we can find out if that's how the old woman got in here."

Hayes followed me to the dock door. He swept the beam of his flashlight over the glaze of snow on the floor. Slate's truck rested against the opening. As Dalton had warned us, the overhead hung open by more than a foot. The tarp he'd used to cover the opening tangled in the open door, and melting snow covered the floor.

"Where did you find the old woman?" Hayes asked.

"There." I pointed. "She was hiding at the bottom of the dumbwaiter shaft."

He shone the flashlight toward the stairway. "Those your tracks?"

"I think so."

Blowing snow had filled in the footprints, but traces of where Shelby and I had walked were faint but plain. Near where I stood was a third, single impression in the snow. It was smaller than the others. The footprint was a child's, and the child was barefoot. I stepped forward and crushed the print under my boots. The child who led us to Eva and lit a candle for us to follow to the warm bed.

"No tellin' when she got in here. She could have hidden down here since sometime last night," I said. "That opening might have saved her. She could have frozen to death."

Hayes shook the snow off the tarp and draped it over the opening. He stepped back, and the next gust of wind tore the tarp away. He watched the tarp flap in the wind.

"Let's go upstairs, Hogan. They'll need our help with

breakfast. And no more questions about Odyssey. People are on edge. You're not going to add to it, Hogan." He tipped his head toward the stairway. "Go ahead."

"You go first. I'll follow you."

Hayes sneered. He leaned the pipe against the wall and went up the stairs.

Chapter 15

Shelby pushed fresh bacon from a platter onto the tray on the steam table. She smiled when she saw me and pursed her lips to blow the stubborn strand of hair off her cheek.

Only four of the twenty tables in the dining room had people. Sugar Kane mixed champagne into mimosa flutes at the bar. Claire placed silverware on the empty tables. Except for the soft sound of champagne bubbles and the clink of the silverware, there was no other noise. No one said a word.

"Where's everybody?"

The smile left Shelby's face. "They don't want to eat breakfast with a dead body in the next room."

"Is that it?"

"I think so. A few have come down and filled a plate, and gone back to their room."

I picked up a plate and scooped up a spoonful of the scrambled eggs. "It's got to be cold up in those rooms," I added bacon and a sticky cinnamon roll to the plate.

"It's cold down here." She shivered. I watched tears well up in her eyes. I set the plate down and stepped around the table to be close to her.

When I reached for her, she pushed my hand away. "Guy, I'm frightened," she whispered.

"It's all right."

"No, it's not." She raised her voice.

Claire lifted her face. At the few tables, heads turned.

I took a deep breath. I felt stupid. "You're right." I searched for something to say. "We just have to—"

"Wait. Like Dalton said. Don't say that again." This time, she reached for me. I took her in my arms. "Guy, I'm cold. I'm tired, and I'm frightened. Tell me something more than we have to wait."

"I—"

She looked up at me.

"I wish there were more."

"So do I."

Sugar Kane stepped up. She held out a mimosa in each hand. "Maybe you can use one of these." She forced a smile.

I took a glass and finished it in a single gulp. Shelby sipped once and toyed with the glass. She caught the edge of her apron and lifted it to dab her eyes. When she looked at me, the fear was gone for now. Not because of a sip of the champagne. Or from anything I said. She was strong. I knew it. Then she smoothed the apron, picked up the empty platter, and her back straightened.

"Dalton said you were in the basement with Hayes."

"He wanted to check the generator."

"Did he say anything?"

"He made it very clear he didn't want to answer any questions about Odyssey. I guess—"

"I know. We have to wait."

Claire raised a finger and pointed at the windows. "Look." She left the silverware on the table and crossed the room. Guests at their tables stood. It wasn't that I saw anything. It was more than I felt the change.

The room was brighter. Shadows moved back.

One of the guests leaned close to the glass. "The snowflakes," he said, "are smaller."

Another woman pointed at the sky. "I think I see the sun."

Sugar Kane was at the window. "The wind's died down. Could the storm end that quickly?"

Dalton pushed his way to join the others. "I lived in the Colorado mountains all my life. We can get this kind of storm sometimes. Comes in quick. Temperatures drop. Snow comes down in waves, and the wind blows like a banshee. Then it just plays itself out."

"What about the electricity?" Sugar's husband asked.

"No tellin'." Dalton hooked his thumbs into his gun belt. "They've got to get the plows out and clear the roads first. I don't know where we are on the list of priorities. But they'll get to us when they get to us."

"Phones?" Doc Kane asked.

"I just checked a few minutes ago," Dalton told him. "Nope. Nothing yet. But the clouds appear to be breakin' up. That's a good sign for all of us."

"Listen. I hear something." Sugar put her finger to her lips. "Hush, everyone, please."

I heard it too.

Chapter 16

I took Shelby's hand and followed Sugar, her husband, and the others to the lobby. A fire blazed in the fireplace, but no one was near it. We joined the dozen people crowded at the front windows.

Stray, small snowflakes drifted in swirls near the building. The landscape was a blend of whites and grays. Not a track, bit of a branch, or a stone marred the blanket of snow. Drifts covered bushes, and snow clumped in the branches of the pine trees as if night had fled and a child's playground of cotton candy pillows had settled before us. High up, cool white rays from the sun found the cracks in the clouds, and everything we could see in the dawn's light glistened like a million diamonds.

"Listen," Sugar pleaded.

Each of us held our breath.

The sound was faint. Only a slight hum from the edge of the white quiet.

"I hear it, too," Dalton whispered.

"There." A woman pointed.

Where the blur of the white horizon met the dull skies, a wispy, different shade of gray lifted.

"What is that?" Doc Kane pointed.

"Smoke?" I guessed.

The hum turned to a growl.

A dark blur crested the horizon. Then another. The sound grew louder.

"Is it a—" Doc Kane squinted. "I think it's a snowmobile."

People leaned closer. Hands pressed against the frosty window.

"No," Shelby said, "there are two of them."

"Coming to save us?" A woman asked.

"Most likely, they're out checkin' to see who needs help after the storm." Dalton pushed away from the group. "Hogan, Hayes, come with me."

We crossed the lobby. Dalton put his back to the front door. "Help me," he said.

Hayes opened the latch. We both pushed on the door. The crusty snow and ice had frozen the door shut.

"Heave," Dalton barked.

I threw my shoulder against the door. I heard Dalton grunt. Hayes kicked at the threshold, and an inch at a time, the door began to break free. We pushed. The sound of the snowmobiles went from a hum to a roar. I slipped through the open gap and kicked away the snow on the porch until the door could swing open. Chunks of snow fell from the building, and bits landed in my hair and onto the collar of my jacket.

Dalton and Hayes joined me on the porch.

The snowmobile's driver revved the engine, and the sled rocketed up the snow-covered stairs. The driver killed the engine, and the quiet replaced the roar. He tugged back his black stocking cap and pushed his snow goggles down.

"Hey, Dalton." The driver nodded at me. "Heard I'd find you and Hogan up here. You all surviving the storm so far?" He looked at me again, then his eyes paused on Hayes.

"Mostly fine, Mike," Dalton told him, "but we got big trouble."

"Don't like the sound of that." Mike Sanchez, Estes Park's police chief, swung his leg over the snowmobile and stood up. "What you got?"

Dalton spoke first. "Dead woman."

"She was murdered," Hayes blurted out. "I saw the one who did it. He ran off in the night. He couldn't have gone far. Did you catch him?"

"Keep your voice down." Sanchez's eyes narrowed, and mist curled from his nostrils. "You know for sure she's dead, Dalton?"

"She's dead." Dalton shook his head.

Sanchez tugged at the zipper of his snowsuit and reached inside. His hand came out with a handheld radio. He turned his back to us and spoke, "Jimmy, we made it here to the hotel. Get in touch with the coroner. Tell 'em we got a body up here. You two figure out the best way to get someone up here. Keep me posted on what you find out. I'll do what I can here." He jammed the radio into his pocket. "Let's go on inside."

The engine of the other snowmobile revved. A rooster-tail of snow rose from the spinning track. Instead of coming to us, its driver cut a wide path away from the hotel.

I pointed. "Where are they going?"

"I told them to make a circle around the hotel to look over things and check the outbuildings before they come on in."

"Looks like there are two of your men on that sled?"

"You're right, Hogan. Now let's get out of this cold."

—

Shelby held out a cup of coffee. Sanchez peeled himself out of his snowmobile suit and took the cup from her hand. He held it so the steam would spread around his fingers before he took the first sip.

He nodded his thanks.

The folks from the lobby crowded around him, and others who must have heard the snowmobiles came down the staircase.

"How much longer 'til we can get out of here?" a man shouted from the stairs.

"Is the storm over?" from another.

"What about the electricity?" A woman pushed closer.

"The phones? I need to contact my offices." It was Periwinkle.

Sanchez raised a hand. "I tell you all know." He gulped down some coffee. "Quiet now." He glanced around the group. "Let's move into the lobby. It will be easier for you all to hear."

The crowd began to move. Hayes tossed an armload of wood onto the fire in the fireplace. He dropped onto one knee, huffed his cheeks, and blew into the ashes. Red glowed, and in seconds flames rose and chased the shadows into the corners of the room.

Sanchez caught my arm and then leaned closer to me. "Hogan, which one is Odyssey Pruit?" he whispered.

I started to speak. I needed to know why he needed Odyssey.

Sanchez shook his head. "Just point to her."

Chapter 17

Chief Sanchez stood with his back to the fireplace. He took a sip from his second cup of coffee. "Let's start with what I can tell you now. There is an order in effect from the governor since six last night. This was one helluva of a storm. All major highways are shut down. Emergency travel only. The county issued shelter-in-place orders. Nobody's going anywhere."

There were murmurs from the people. Sanchez lifted a hand. "You heard me. You're stuck here until that order is rescinded. Sorry. There's nothin' I can do about it." He looked around the room as if he wanted to be sure each had heard. "Now for the good news. The National Weather Service is reporting that the storm is moving east. They expect clearing here in Estes by midday with rising temperatures." The murmur turned to relief. Again, Sanchez lifted his hands. "That sounds good, but there's two and a half feet of snow out there. And more than that in the drifts. City plows are out. County's, too. The Highway Department is starting on the major roads, but it's going to take some time."

"When will they get to us?"

"Their first priority is getting a way cleared to the hospital. Then we'll start working on the other roads. No good guess on when they'll get here."

"And the power and the phones?" Dalton asked.

"It's spotty. Some of the stores downtown have power. Across the street, it's black. They're trying to get things going, but it's the same story. I know it sounds harsh, but they'll get here when they get here. I don't know how else to say it."

The fire sputtered. With a crack, a spark popped from a burning log and landed on the hearth. I spotted Odyssey on one of the couches. Ms. Randolph was next to her. Odyssey seemed very small. The older woman held her hand.

"Now, about the dead woman," Sanchez said. For the first time, the murmurs quieted. "Dalton filled me in with what he knows. The boys downtown are trying to get word to the coroner's office."

The radio in his pocket chirped. Sanchez put it to his ear. Static squawked. "Give me more time. I call you when I need you," he said to the radio and turned back to us. "Shelby said they're keeping breakfast warm. I'd like everyone to get something to eat now. If you have already eaten or aren't hungry, I need you to go to your rooms. There's police business I need to attend to." He narrowed his eyes and looked the people over again. "You heard me."

Folks got up from where they had been listening. Some went to the windows for a moment as if to see if what Sanchez said about the storm was true. Others headed back upstairs. Most went to the restaurant.

Sanchez stepped up to me. "Which one is Odyssey?"

I tipped my head towards the woman as the crowd moved away. Sanchez took a glance. "Thought so," he whispered.

"What's this about? Why Odyssey?"

"Like everything else, Hogan. You're gonna hafta wait." He tuned and called Dalton. "You got the keys?" He pointed his chin across the lobby.

"Hayes has them," Dalton answered.

"You and Hayes come with me. You too, Hogan."

—

The fire in the fireplace was dying, and as the clouds hid the sun, the lobby darkened.

"You said the body's in the Billiard Room?" Sanchez asked. "Which one of those doors?" He turned to Jim Hayes.

Hayes pointed. "It's the door on the left."

"And the other door?"

"That's the Piano Room. It's where the paintings are set up for the auction."

"This Odyssey Pruit is the artist?"

"Yeah."

"And the dead woman?"

"Her manager, Porsche Hurt."

Sanchez squinted as if he was storing away each of the answers to his questions. "Can you get from one room to the other without having to come through the lobby?"

"Yeah, there's a door at the back. The staff uses it to set the room or serve during an event." Hayes rubbed his hands together and looked at me, then Dalton, and finally back to Sanchez.

A chill drifted across the room.

"Do you keep those rooms locked?"

"The lobby doors are kept locked unless there's an event."

"Were they locked last night?

"They should have been."

"Who has the keys?" Sanchez looked at Hayes.

"I've got a master key. I can use it to get into the Billiard Room."

"What about the Piano Room? You don't have a key for that?"

Hayes shook his head. "Shelby was the liaison for the Art

Show and Auction, so she would have had the key to that room."

"Your master doesn't work for the Piano Room?"

Jim Hayes tugged at his collar. "No." He looked down at the floor. "Why all these questions?"

"Get used to it, Hayes. We're in the middle of a death investigation. You're going to have to answer these questions several more times before this is through. Now, last question before I have a look at the body. The side door you mentioned? Was it locked last night?"

"Ask Hogan." Hayes looked at me. "It should have been."

Sanchez turned my way. His eyebrows arched. "Hogan?"

"Ah. Um." I swallowed and tried to find the right words. How could I explain Betsy leading us to Eva? "Ah. I helped Shelby and the others unpack and set up the pictures for the auction. Shelby and I were the last to leave. We put the empty crates and boxes just inside that side door. That was about one o'clock. I remember Shelby locking the lobby door, but I can't be sure about the side door. I don't remember if Shelby locked it. You'll need to ask her."

Hayes raised his voice. "And you and Shelby came back later. Tell him that. And you haven't let me tell you what I saw. It was that truck driver, Slate. Hogan saw him, too."

"Just laying the groundwork. I need to go slow and get an understanding." Sanchez ran his fingers through his crew cut. "I've done this too many times. I still don't like it. Show me the body."

Dalton pushed the door open. Thick curtains covered the windows, and the wooden floor creaked under our weight. Sunlight from the clearing clouds hadn't found the Billiard Room. It was icy cold, and chills ran up my back. I didn't want to see the body again.

What had Odyssey said? "It's not just a dead body. Why won't anyone say her name? She's Porsche."

I stared at the floor. I didn't want to see Porsche again.

Sanchez turned on his flashlight and probed the dark room.

He swept the light over the walls and then the floor, staying away from the corner where Porsche, not the body, lay.

"Dalton," he called, "Light. You two"—he nodded and Hayes and me—"wait here."

Dalton took two steps forward, switched on his flashlight, and trained the beam on Porsche's dead body. Sanchez slipped his radio from his pocket, thumbed the switch, and raised it to his mouth. "You two head on in here." And he kneeled near Porsche's head. "Whattya think, Dalton?"

Dalton hunkered down on his heels beside Sanchez. He pointed his flashlight at the woman. "See the bruises on her throat?"

Sanchez nodded.

"I'm thinkin' whoever it was slipped up on her from behind, grabbed her, and either strangled her or snapped her neck. It's hard to see in the dark, but I didn't see any signs of a struggle around the body. I think he broke her neck. It was over quick. At least, I hope so."

From outside, the sound of the other snowmobile grew louder. We turned to listen.

"What's that?" Hayes asked.

"I told those two to finish up outside and head on in and warm up," Sanchez told us. He stood and stepped away from the body. Dalton followed him.

Sanchez nodded to Dalton. Both men switched off their flashlights. Shadows spread, and the darkness turned velvety. The gray light from the lobby spread through the open door. I could see Sanchez and Dalton, but their faces disappeared in the dark. Hayes moved back until he was silhouetted in the lobby doorframe.

"Jim?" Sanchez used his first name. "I know you saw some things last night. Start from the beginning. Go slow and don't leave anything out."

"I was in the lobby. The clock had just struck once. It must have been one thirty. This door was open. I thought it was strange. I started to walk over to shut the door when I saw a light from a flashlight. Coming from in here."

"Why were you in the lobby at that time of night?"

"Couldn't sleep." Hayes looked at me. "There were some people in the hall upstairs. A kid with a toy car caused some excitement. After that settled down, I just couldn't sleep. I'm responsible for these people, you know. So, I came downstairs to check on things."

"What things?" Sanchez was quick with the question.

"I don't know. Just couldn't sleep. Thought I'd walk around and check the doors. Make sure no one else was wandering around. Check the kitchen. Those kinds of things."

"Go on."

"Anyway, I saw the light in here. Then I heard people."

"You heard voices?"

"Not so much. More like I heard the struggle."

"And?"

"I was at the door." He pointed. "I saw the woman on the floor. Slate was kneeling over her. He had her on the floor, and his hands were on her throat."

"Slate?"

Hayes fidgeted. He shifted from one foot to the other. "The truck driver who brought the artwork. He got stuck in the snow. Stranded like the rest of us."

"It was dark in here. Just the light from a flashlight, you said. You sure it was Slate?"

"I saw his braids."

"Braids?" Sanchez stepped out of the shadows.

"Yeah, braids. Slate has this long hair. Braids. Like Willie Nelson. Those kind of braids."

"So, you're sure it was Slate?"

"Positive." Hayes's eyes darted my way. "Ask Hogan."

"I'll get to Hogan in a minute. Tell me what happened next."

"I must have yelled something. Slate jumped up from her and pushed by me. Ran out the door. That's when Hogan must have seen him."

"Anything else?"

Hayes shook his head.

The sound of the snowmobile faded. The front door whined on its hinges and then slammed shut. Boots stomped off the snow.

Hayes took another step back. He glanced out the doorway. "Hogan came in and tried to save her. But it was too late." Hayes moved into a swatch of shadows. The back staircase was behind him. "What about Slate? Did you catch him? Is he out there in the snow?"

"You see, Jim." Sanchez flipped on his flashlight. Yellow light blended with the shadows. "I got a message yesterday to call the Des Moines Police Department. A detective wanted to talk to me about a missing woman."

"What's this got to do with—"

"Hear me out." Sanchez rubbed his chin. "I got a hold of the detective just as it started to snow last night. He told me a family reported their daughter missing about six months ago. They're concerned. I can understand that. But the woman is an adult. Adults can lose themselves if they want. But the family has been searching. The daughter is something of an artist. But she's challenged. A bit slow, if you know what I mean. They're afraid someone might take advantage of her."

Footsteps clomped across the lobby floor.

Hayes looked from one side to the other. He strained to see Sanchez's men in the lobby.

"The family saw something that made them think their girl was here in Estes. I promised I'd look into it. By then, it was snowing hard, and I had a lot of things to get done."

"I don't understand what this has to do—"

The figures of two men filled the doorway. In the backlight, the first pulled off the hood from his parka. Dark braids tumbled free.

"It's him," Slate shouted. "I saw him drag that woman in

here." He pointed a gloved hand at Hayes. "He was choking her. I saw him."

Confusion swarmed. It crawled over me like a thousand ants. Breath caught in my lungs.

Slate was at the center of the room. Sanchez pointed his flashlight in Hayes's face. Hayes stepped back. "It's his word against mine," he shouted. "I'm telling you I saw him kill her."

"Liar." Slate lunged for Hayes.

I caught Slate's arm. But he was strong. He broke free and threw a wild punch at Hayes's stomach.

Hayes dodged the punch. He snatched a pool stick from a wall rack, cocked it behind his shoulder, and swung for Slate's face.

Slate's scream and the sound of tearing flesh and crunching bone became one. Slate fell to the floor, hands clutching his ruined face. Hayes vaulted the first billiard table and lunged for the doorway to the steep back stairs.

Flashlight beams bobbed up and down with Sanchez's running steps. Dalton was close behind. The two kneeled behind a billiard table near the door. Even in the gray half-light, I could see that Dalton had his gun in his hand.

"What's back there?" Sanchez hollered. "Can he get outside?"

"The stairs go down to the loading dock." I crouched behind the nearest table. "They're steep. If he makes it down, he can get out of the building."

"Is there another way down there?" Sanchez asked Dalton.

"Yeah. I'm goin'." Dalton hurried by me, and then out into the lobby, headed for the other stairs.

Slate moaned. The other policeman moved to him.

"How bad?" Sanchez called.

"It's bad," the cop yelled back.

"Can you drag him to the lobby?"

"On our way, boss." The cop grabbed Slate's coat collar and dragged him out of the Billiard Room.

My heart thumped in my ears, and breath rasped up my throat. I moved so that I could peek at the closed door to the back stairway.

"Hayes?" Sanchez called. "Come on out. It's no use. You've got nowhere to go."

"I'll come out. Don't shoot me. It was Slate, I tell ya. Don't shoot."

"I won't hurt you. Push open the door. Hands up so I can see you."

"Okay, okay. Just don't shoot."

Sanchez's flashlight lit the door. The door swung open, and Hayes stood in the opening. He raised his hands, squinted, and turned his face in the glare from the flashlight.

"Turn around. Hand on your head."

Hayes did what he was told.

"Take two steps back. Don't turn around." Sanchez stood up. He was a black inkblot against the shadows. He holstered his gun and slipped a pair of handcuffs from his belt. The flashlight never left Hayes.

"It's over," I told myself and lifted my head above the tabletop.

Sanchez stepped around the billiard table. "Don't move," he ordered. Flashlight held high, he moved forward. One hand found Hayes's hand on the top of his head. He took Hayes's wrist.

Tension eased out of me.

But Hayes wrenched his arm away. He turned to face Sanchez and shoved him back. Sanchez sprawled backwards onto the floor. From the edge of the doorframe, Hayes snatched the pool stick and slammed it down across the policemen's shins.

With everything in me, I threw myself across the room. Screams of Hayes's anger and Sanchez's pain filled the room. Hayes raised the stick to strike again. I launched myself at him.

My shoulder caught him just above his belt. Breath

whooshed from him. The stick clattered onto the dark floor. Everything was black. His fingers gouged my eyes. I swung wildly, fist connecting with his face. Hayes stumbled back onto the landing above the dumbwaiter. He fell back onto the railing. Wood splintered.

For an instant, he hung over the black nothing. His mouth opened, but there was no sound. Then he was falling. I lunged, belly down on the floor, I reached to save him. Our hands touched.

Then, he was gone.

Dalton's flashlight lit the little space at the bottom. Twenty-one steps from where I lay to Hayes's twisted body. It was where Shelby and I found Eva. Brown had told the story of the little whore that fell here, and I thought of the woman who listened to her die.

Dalton touched Hayes's neck. Blood pooled around Hayes' face.

Dalton looked up at me. He shook his head.

Chapter 18

Shelby wrapped an icicle she'd snapped from the building in a towel and laid it across Sanchez's legs. He winced and leaned back on the couch in front of the lobby's fireplace.

Outside, the tractor's blade scraped snow from the rough pavement. The sun was shining, and rivulets of melting snow crisscrossed the lobby's windows. The last ambulance—the one with Porsche and Hayes—rolled over the packed snow to the plowed roads and the highway.

Shelby sat on the arm of the couch beside me. She touched the gouged places on my cheek with a cold towel.

"Slate stumbled into our office downtown, half-frozen." Sanchez went on. "We got him some coffee and wrapped him in a blanket. He starts goin' on about how he saw Hayes murder that woman. It's a miracle he didn't freeze to death in the storm. And how he found his way to us in the blowing snow, I'll never know."

Dalton's eyes were red-rimmed. He joined us on the couch and rubbed his forehead. Drops of Hayes's blood still stained his jeans. He rested his head in his hands.

"The EMT says anything about Slate's face?" Shelby asked.

Dalton looked up. "He was sure he had a concession. Nose was half tore off. Lost some teeth. They were making arrangements for a plastic surgeon at the hospital in Fort Collins as they left here. Slate's gonna make it, but it's gonna take time."

I felt Hayes's hand slip through my fingers again, and I heard his bones shatter on the cement floor. I shuddered at the memories. Shelby turned my face to hers. She squeezed my hand.

I had to say it. "What happened here?"

Sanchez leaned forward. He shifted the towel-covered ice on his legs. "I can tell you what I know and what I pieced together, but I can't explain it."

"I have to know something."

"From what the detective in Iowa said, it comes together something like this. Odyssey's real name is Marion. She grew up in a small town outside Des Moines. Didn't finish high school, lived with her parents, where she could hold a job—she gathered shopping carts in the Walmart parking lot or cleaned up spills on the floors. That kind of stuff. Since she was a kid, she liked to paint pictures."

Sanchez leaned back. "That Randolph woman, and that's not her real name, crosses paths with this Marion at some flea market somewhere. She sees these pictures Marion, or Odyssey, is selling, and the wheels start turning. The two get friendly. Pretty soon, Marion moves in with Randolph. Somewhere along the line, Randolph gets in touch with Hayes."

Shelby squeezed my hand. "So, Ms. Randolph knew Hayes? She worked here at the hotel, like we guessed?"

"Yeah. You found that picture," Sanchez said.

"Where does Porsche Hurt fit into all this?" I asked.

"Somebody a lot smarter than me is going to have to figure that out. This is what I understand. Porsche isn't what you thought she was."

"How so?"

Sanchez stretched. He winced when he moved his leg. "Porsche Hurt, and that's her real name, believe it or not."

Dalton huffed through his mustache.

Sanchez grinned. "According to the detective, Porsche is in the art business. Never amounted to anything big. She's living well on alimony from two exes. But she had some contacts and knew some of the right people. The detective's not sure if she was part of the scheme or if her eyes got big and she just got greedy."

"And why did Hayes—"

Sanchez shrugged. "Kill her? We'll never know. I'm guessing money. Somebody wanted more? The other wouldn't give in. Which one was which?" He shrugged again. "You know the hell of it? There's no crime."

Shelby's mouth dropped open. Dalton sat up.

"He might be right," I said. "Think about it. Hayes murdered Porsche. He's dead. Even if the forensic evidence points to him. He's dead. And the pictures—there won't be an auction, so Stephen King and Michael Jackson, and all the others won't be cheated out of their money."

"Ms. Randolph and Odyssey?" Shelby said, "There must be something."

Sanchez shook his head. "I guess Randolph clammed up and isn't saying a word. She claims she's got some high-dollar lawyer. And Odyssey? Even if she was a part of the scheme, she might not be competent to stand trial."

A ledge of snow broke free from the roof and splattered on the ground outside.

"The hotel was to be paid out of the auction proceeds." Shelby laughed. "There goes my commission. But"—her face turned serious—"Those things we heard late at night." She looked at me. "How frightened we were? What about that?"

"Maybe they won."

Chapter 19

Afternoon sunlight flooded in from every window. The fire in the fireplace had burned out. I tugged my jacket off. Doc Kane and Sugar walked into the lobby.

"We're headed out," he said. "I left our information with your officer. Don't hesitate to contact us if you need anything," he told Sanchez.

Doc Kane shook my hand. "What an adventure. We'll have stories to tell our children about all this." He smiled at Sugar.

Sugar tapped her tummy. "Uh-huh." She beamed.

Shelby stood, and the two women hugged.

"See you in the summer. Hogan, you promised to take me fishing." He wrapped his arm around Sugar, and they left us.

Others joined. Claire brought Eva.

"Eva has something she'd like to tell you." Claire sat on the arm of the couch. Eva sat next to Shelby.

After a minute, Shelby straightened the blanket over Eva's shoulders. "C'mon." She helped Eva stand and took her hand. "Walk with me."

"Where are we going?" Eva whispered to Shelby.

"To talk with Mister Hogan."

"I like him. He helped me when I was cold."

Shelby wrapped her arm around Eva's bent shoulders. The two moved from the couch to where I stood near the fireplace.

"Eva, tell Mister Hogan what you told Claire."

Eva lifted her face. "My birthday?" A strange smile curled at her mouth.

"Yes, Eva, when's your birthday?"

Tears filled the old woman's eyes. She seemed to look at me and nowhere at all.

"November," Eva whispered. "November first."

"So, tomorrow is your birthday?" I held out my hand. Eva took my fingers with both her hands. "Happy Birthday, Eva."

"What year were you born?" Shelby coaxed.

Eva turned her head and peered at Shelby. "Go ahead, Eva. Tell Mister Hogan."

"Nineteen..." She looked up at me. "November first, nineteen-o-nine."

I did the calculations. "You'll turn seventy-three tomorrow."

Eva tilted her head.

"Tell me why you came to this old hotel?"

"My sister," she whispered, "wanted me to come."

I bent down. "What about your sister?"

"She told me."

"What did she tell you?" Shelby spoke softly.

"I was too little to remember." Eva brightened. She squeezed my finger tighter. The icy cold left, and my warmth moved into her hands. "Sister told me. We stayed upstairs. There were other children. We rode ponies, took walks in the woods. Went fishing." A laugh escaped her mouth. "Sister said I caught the biggest."

"What else?"

"We played tag on the stairs with the others. Hide and seek in the halls. Sister told me how much fun we had. Played tricks on the maid." Her nose wrinkled like a little girl's.

"Where's your sister now?"

Eva's face darkened. "Sick. So sick. Mommy said the angels took her. I cried. We never came back here again." Then she smiled. "But sister did."

I looked at Shelby. "Brown's story?" I mouthed. Shelby nodded. "Tell Mister Hogan your sister's name."

She giggled, and tears ran down her cheeks. "I called her Sister. But her name was Betsy."

A lump rose in my throat. I tried to make words, but no words would form in my mouth.

There were tears on Shelby's cheeks. "Where's Sister now?"

Eva raised her arm. Her hand trembled. She pointed a filthy, twisted finger. "That room. Where the piano is. Sister said we weren't even supposed to touch it. But I did. I got my fingers slapped."

"Betsy's in there now?" I asked softly.

"Yes." Eva's face brightened. "Sister is in the room with the big piano. Now."

—

"Mike." I found Sanchez at the registration desk. "We need to get into the Piano Room."

"I told you, Hogan. It's part of the crime scene. No one goes in there until the crime scene boys from the state get up here and do their thing. Like I told you before, I have no idea when they'll get here."

Outside, the snow glistened in the sun. The driver of the city's tractor pulled off his hat and gloves and lowered his head. He waited at the foot of the drive as Doc Kane's car crept down the single plowed lane and rumbled onto the snow-packed highway.

"Please, Mike. It's for the old woman. She's upset." It was a half-truth. I needed to see what was in the room. Or who.

"Thought you said Doctor Kane said she was all right. Just

needed to rest."

"Physically, she's probably okay. She's agitated. After all she's been through. She's sure her sister is in the room." I said nothing about a little girl ghost named Betsy. "Just let us open the door. She'll see her sister's not there. It'll calm her down, then she can rest."

The chandelier above my head flickered on. The elevator groaned with its first hint of electricity. The cash register at the registration desk chimed, and people cheered.

The few still gathered there looked up. At first, there was a hush. Then, people began to laugh.

The sheriff's shoulders eased. "Guess that's a good sign."

The tractor outside started its second pass up the narrow driveway. Black smoke belched over the snow-covered cars. Chunks of snow flew into the air.

"What about it, Mike? Let the woman look."

He shook his head. "Who's got a key?"

I looked across the lobby. Shelby raised her head.

—

Some part of me wanted the ghost of a child to welcome her aged sister. Other parts wanted the room to be just as we left it. I wanted to see easels of Odyssey's strange art and the open lid of a grand piano. Eva held my hand. I closed my eyes as Shelby turned the key.

Then Eva tugged on my hand. Shelby gasped.

Every crystal on the chandelier over the piano sparked. The curtains were open. It was so different from the dark room at midnight.

Then I saw the pictures. Some had tumbled from the easels. Others were covered with childish handprints of garish paint. The picture of Betsy and the man in my boots had been slashed corner to corner.

Only the wrapped picture behind the piano seemed untouched.

"Don't go in there, Hogan," Sanchez shouted.

It was too late. Eva had my hand. We hurried around the piano. The picture leaned against the wall, and it was still wrapped in brown paper.

I reached out and tore the paper away.

The canvas was blank. Not a brush had dared touch it. Not a bit of paint anywhere. I stood and gawked. Confused by what was before me.

But Eva tugged on my hand. She pointed and covered his mouth with her hands. She laughed like a little girl.

At the bottom corner. The one closest to Eva, in a childish scrawl, was the words "happy birthday.".

Chapter 20

Shelby rested her forehead on my shoulder. She yawned and looked up at me. "Happy Halloween, Guy. I'm going to sleep forever."

"I might never sleep again."

"But it's over."

"Is it?"

"We did everything we could. Our part's over."

"Maybe you're right. Now what?"

She blew the stubborn lock of hair off her cheek. "I want to meet Zac."

"Huh?"

"Zac. Your beagle. You promised that I could meet him."

"You will."

"I'm taking tomorrow off."

"Then tomorrow you'll meet Zac."

She smiled. I did too.

"Dalton is ready to get going. He's anxious to get home. And tomorrow I promise."

I met Dalton on the front porch.

He tipped his Stetson down and squinted at the glare off the pure white snow. "They're calling this the Storm of the Century, Hogan." Wisps of steam rose from the sidewalk between his boots. "Heck, I've been through six, maybe seven, storms of the century. This is just another one. It was barely zero last night, and it's near forty degrees now. All this snow will be gone by midweek. It's just the way nature chooses to do things."

I slung my duffel bag over my shoulder and stepped around a puddle of fresh-melted snow on the warm sidewalk. "What about everything that happened to us? They took two dead people out of here. How do you explain that? Is that what nature chose to do?"

Dalton stopped and looked up at the sky. "Hardly a cloud anywhere." He turned to me. "You and me will never know why people like Hayes and that Randolph woman did what they did. And the other part? I told you the world was off-kilter. We all felt it. Was it because of the storm, the dark, the cold, no phones, no power? Did we conjure up something that wasn't there?"

"But what about—"

He cut me off. "The tapping sound in the downstairs hallway. Water from a leaky pipe. Eva put a plate on the floor to catch the runoff. That one was easy."

"What about—"

"Little boy's toy car. Sounds from the wind. Old stairs creak. Maybe people wanted something that wasn't there."

I wanted more. I wanted to know.

A spray of snow cascaded from the branches of the tall pine where I had found Odyssey's rabbit. Was it just yesterday? It seemed days, not hours, ago. A shadow swept over the white snow.

Dalton whistled through his teeth. He pointed. "A big ole owl out to find something to eat after the storm. You know an owl that size can pluck the head off a cottontail as slick as can be. They leave the body behind and fly off and eat the brains. You'd swear some cut the head off with a pair of scissors. It's that clean."

"You mean?"

We both looked up to watch the owl. The eaves shaded a window on the fourth floor. Water dripped from the melting snow, and the breeze teased the window's curtain. Steamy mist covered the glass. Two tiny hands touched the glass and left handprints on the haze.

"Dalton?"

"I didn't see that either, Hogan. I didn't see it either."

Author's Note

Early Snow presented a different challenge than other stories I have written. *The Homeplace* is set in the farm and ranch country of the Eastern Colorado plains. In *The Bootheel*, a teenage orphan cowboy and an old gunman follow a treasure map through the deserts of Mexico. In the first Guy Hogan mystery, *Trailridge*, readers are introduced to the rivers, forests, mountains, and the twists and turns of Trail Ridge Road. While the elements of a mountain blizzard are very much a part of *Early Snow*, the story happens indoors. How did I do?

Thanks to so many who helped me write this story. Valued friends from Rocky Mountain Fiction Writers, my Monday night Zoom group, and my long-suffering wife, and special thanks to Suzie Q. You're the best.

I plan to share the next Guy Hogan Mystery in 2026. Watch my website for details. www.kevinwolfstoryteller.com

Author's Note on *Belthanger*

My grandfather was a traveling salesman for a large automobile parts wholesaler during the 1930s and 1940s. He called on auto parts stores, large fleets, and government shops on Colorado's eastern plains. He told wonderful stories about his travels, and one of those stories was the inspiration for *Belthanger*.

The owner of one auto parts store was an accomplished rifleman. He won turkey shoots at the county fairs, friendly competitions, and always got his deer. My grandfather wove a wonderful story of fleeing bank robbers. Word came that the outlaws were toward the town where the rifleman had his store. The state police positioned the rifleman in the upstairs window of his parts store with orders to take a shot at the escaping bad guys.

I thought about this story for years, did some investigations, and have come to conclude that my grandfather made the whole thing up.

In 2021, Western Writers of America selected *Belthanger* as the Spur Award winner for best short fiction. I hope you enjoy the story.

BELTHANGER

Paul Townsend gripped the edge of the rough wooden window frame on the second floor of his father's auto parts store. He pulled up until the window broke free of twenty years of old paint and petrified bird droppings.

Paul knew night came to the prairie first. Out there, where the edge of town met the pastures and crop ground, day faded and dark came all at once. On the streets of Kingdom, night came slower. Porch lights, the neon from the drugstore sign, and the pulse of the town's only stoplight battled the night until the dark settled like a fever on a sick bed.

This one time, he wanted night to come in a hurry.

A hint of exhaust from the street below and the sweet-sick smell of the feedlot mixed with the stale air in the cramped room. Paul pushed a case of quart cans of thirty-weight motor oil against the wall beneath the window and stacked another on top of it. He found the chair his father wouldn't throw away in the corner of the room, wiped years of dust from the seat, and slid it behind the boxes.

"You listen to me, Paulie." The sheriff swiped a wrinkled handkerchief across his face. Shadows stretched across the room and painted the walls with figures of men ten feet tall.

"My name's Paul." He turned so he could see the sheriff. "You call me Paul," he said, "not Paulie, and never call me Belthanger ever again."

The sheriff mashed on a toothpick in the corner of his mouth. "This won't be the turkey shoot at the county fair, and it won't be anything like those prairie dogs, Paul. If I say so, you're gonna be shootin' a man."

The room was so quiet, it was loud, and all Paul knew was after tonight nobody would call him Belthanger ever again

From the staircase outside the door, a voice called, "Sheriff, the Courtesy Patrol's on the phone. They need to talk to you right now."

The sheriff hooked his thumbs in his belt and tugged his pants up his belly. "Deputy Barker and I need to go downstairs. You think over what we just talked about."

Yesterday's burned tobacco, the sweat in the pits of their uniform shirts and the Old Spice that they had splashed on their faces that morning left the room with the two lawmen. The steps creaked under the big sheriff. Each board played its own sounds. The fifth step from the top groaned the loudest.

Outside, a farmer's truck full of new wire and fence posts waited for the stoplight to change. Mrs. Potter came out of the front door of her husband's Rexall and waddled across the street to the bank. Paul checked his Timex. It was ten minutes to six o'clock. The same time she had made the trip every day for the past eighteen years.

He slipped his Winchester from its sheepskin case, took the red shop rag from his back pocket and wiped the smudges of his own fingerprints from the blued steel.

The stoplight changed to green, and the farmer's truck started for home. The bank's door shut behind Mrs. Potter's wide rump.

He laid the Winchester on the oil cases. The stoplight would change in three minutes and eleven seconds. Like it did every day, two hundred and twenty-two times. From when he turned the key in the front door in the morning until Big Paul turned off the store lights at night.

—

The sheriff looked at the phone in his hand for a long second before he hung up. He dug into his shirt pocket, plucked a cinnamon toothpick from its wax paper and hung a new one in the corner of his mouth.

"Jeffery, you get down to Farson's." The sheriff rubbed his temple as if to coax a thought free. "Have Earl get that big flatbed they use to haul lumber. You tell him I want him to park it right out there like it's stopped at the light." He tipped the top of his head to where Front Avenue crossed Main Street. "Have him put the hood up, so's folks'll think it's broke down."

The sheriff mopped the sweat from the folds in his thick neck. He waited until Jeffery was out the door. "It's worse than they told us, Barker. Patrol says he's got a hostage in the car. Made one of the tellers leave with him."

"Damn, Sheriff," Barker whispered.

He moved the toothpick from one side of his mouth to the other. "Get on upstairs and see what Belthang—I mean Paul—is thinkin'. Don't say nothin' about the hostage. As soon as Jeffery gets back here with that truck, I want the two of you to tell every shopkeeper on Front to turn their lights off. Then do the same thing on Main Street. I want this town as dark as a tomb. Have folks go home and wait 'til we tell them it's all clear. I want the red and green from that stoplight to be the only thing that outlaw sees."

"Shouldn't we talk to Belt's father about this?" Barker asked. "Belt never does anything without Big Paul tellin' him it's all right." The deputy shook his head. "Where is Big Paul anyways?"

"It's Thursday. Big Paul always makes his run to Denver on Thursdays. That's why Paulie has on that necktie today. Big Paul's probably stoppin' at the café about now. After he finishes his apple pie, he'll start for home. Every Thursday he gets back to Kingdom just before ten thirty. Paulie'll take that tie off, unload the truck and get that broomstick with the wire taped to the end and start hanging the fan belts and hoses on the wall. Same thing every Thursday."

"I don't like it one bit, Sheriff." Barker shook his head. "Can this even work?"

"I'm not sure of anything right now. I don't know why that man would rob a bank and drive towards Denver instead of haulin' ass for the Kansas line. But as fast as they say he's drivin'-- he'll be here in Kingdom before the state police can catch him. That stoplight outside is about the only thing that might slow him down. And if it does, Belthanger, up there might just have time to take a shot."

"I don't know, Sheriff. Belt won't miss, but he's not... you know." Barker looked up the stairs. "Belt's different... His father never really let him think for himself."

"Maybe that bank robber will run his car into the ditch. He might turn down any of the dozen county roads between here and there. He might stop and just give up. Or he might drive right down Kingdom's Mainstreet" The sheriff wiped the kerchief over his forehead again. "And Barker, the hostage—" the sheriff coughed into his handkerchief "—it's Alice Tuttle."

"Alice Tuttle?" The deputy cocked his head. "Didn't your brother's daughter marry that Tuttle boy?"

—

Night stole away the blue sky. Through the rifle scope, Paul's eye gathered what light remained. He let the crosshairs rest on the base of Mrs. Potter's neck—-just where her gray hair touched the collar of her flowery dress. He sucked in a breath, blew the air from lungs and tightened his finger on the trigger.

"Bang," he whispered.

Mrs. Potter jiggled from the street to the sidewalk and swayed on her high-heeled shoes for the few steps to the door of the Rexall Drug Store. She tugged her sweater tight around her and reached for the door handle.

The fifth stair step groaned. Boot heels clicked on the sixth stair and didn't stop until Deputy Barker walked into the storeroom. Paul leaned his rifle on the window frame and rested his hands in his lap.

Barker tipped back his Stetson and ran his fingers through his dark hair. "Why don't you loosen that collar and take off the tie?" he asked.

Paul tapped the oil case with the blunt toe of his Montgomery Ward's work shoes. "I can do it," he said. "Shoot him, I mean. I won't miss."

"Sheriff said it might not come to it. That outlaw might not even make it this far."

Paul stared at Barker. "I know I can do it. What is it? Forty yards from this window to the stoplight? I killed that buck deer at two hundred and eighty-three long steps last fall. I can do it."

"Nobody's saying you can't, Belt. Everybody knows you're the best shot in town. Maybe the whole county. I just said he might not make it this far, that's all."

Paul turned back to the window. "Don't you call me Belthanger," he muttered.

"I didn't mean anything by it. You know that. It's just that, since we were kids, seems like you're always in your daddy's store with that stick in your hands, reaching up and hangin' them fan belts on the wall. Half the town don't even know your name's Paul. Everybody calls you Belthanger."

"Don't call me that. It's Paul. Not Paulie. Not Little Paul, either." He leaned forward and rested his elbows on the cardboard box and pretended the rifle was in his hands. He picked at a scab in the crease of his elbow and then made a fist near his cheek. His top finger curled around an imaginary trigger.

"You act like you want this to happen." Barker waited for Paulie to answer.

Instead, Paul's chest swelled with his next breath. His shirt pulled tight across his shoulders, a puff of dust rose from the box as he exhaled, and Paul's finger slowly squeezed. Outside the stoplight clicked and changed from red to green.

"It probably won't happen, I tell ya'. Nothing ever happens in Kingdom. You know that. Next year they're going to start building that interstate highway, and when it's done, most people won't even know this town is here. You listenin' to me?"

Paul waited for the stoplight to change.

The deputy's voice bounced off the walls of the empty room. "Since I hired on, the only time I even took my gun out of its holster was to kill that cow that old man Gray hit with his truck. Remember, every school kid in town ran down to the sale barn that day just to see a dead cow?"

Paul shut his left eye and took aim through the make-believe riflescope. In his mind, the robber had a red bandana tied over his nose and mouth. The man's left arm hung out of the car's window, and a big silver pistol waved in his hand. Bags of money spilled hundred-dollar bills onto the car seat. The car sped down Kingdom's Main Street. The robber looked up at the open window where Paul sat with his deer rifle.

Paulie squeezed the imaginary trigger.

Nobody will call me Belthanger ever again.

—

The light on the steeple of the Front Street Methodist Church went dark. As if a signal, porch lights on the side streets flicked off, pole lights in yards faded, and window curtains pulled shut over darkened living rooms. It was as if his town was dying around him, and it made the sheriff think of ghosts.

The phone jangled on the parts store counter. His meaty hand snatched the phone on the first ring. "Sheriff here."

Words crackled through the phone lines. "The car just passed the Chambers' farm."

"Judas Priest, that's twelve miles from here. You told me he was a half hour away."

"We're piecing the information together as we get it. That's what we know now."

The sheriff slammed his fist on the counter. "I got the boy and his deer rifle in the window. If he's got a shot, do I tell him to take it?"

"It's your call."

He blew air through his teeth. "What about my niece? She still in the car?"

"She's in the passenger seat. We think he blindfolded her, but we're not sure."

The lawman's shoulders slumped, and he tugged at his pants with his free hand.

"Sheriff," the voice hissed through the wire, "he'll be in Kingdom in ten minutes. We have two patrol cars behind him, and we're sending two more your way, but they won't get there before he does. It's your call. Keep someone close to this phone, and we'll let you know if anything changes." The voice on the line hesitated. "And Sheriff, good luck."

The sheriff plucked a new toothpick from his pocket and jammed it in the corner of his mouth. Storefronts on Main Street went dark. Across the street, the barmaid at the Plainsman turned the switch on the neon Coors sign, and the colors wisped into the night. In the Rexall, Mrs. Potter flicked off the display light over the candy counter where he bought his toothpicks. She followed her husband into the storeroom at the back of their store and pulled the door shut behind her. The bright slash of light under the door went dark.

So dark that the Sheriff felt all alone.

—

Paul rolled the rifle cartridge in his fingers. He'd loaded it himself. Poured in the powder one grain at a time and then pressed the copper jacketed bullets into the brass case. The lead-tipped bullets were as sharp as a schoolteacher's pencil, and he wrote his name—not Belthanger-- on the cardboard box with the bullet's soft lead tip.

On the street corner below, Jeffery pulled the front door to the bank building closed, and a man in a white shirt and dark tie shut the blinds and locked the glass door from the inside.

Farson's truck sat in the intersection under the traffic light. It was the only car on Main Street. In a splash of moonlight, the three-legged dog that hung around the gas station did his business in the alley behind the bank.

Only the stoplight gave Kingdom light. The whole town breathed with each change. Inhale on green. Exhale on yellow and hold on red.

The stairs creaked under the Sheriff and the big man huffed for his next breath. Paul scooted his rear end around to face the door.

"I can do it, Sheriff. I know I can."

The armpits of the sheriff's shirt were dark, and the sweat made wet lines where his shirt wrinkled on his belly. "You listen to every word I tell you."

The Sheriff's jaw muscles bunched. He ground on the toothpick stub in the corner of his mouth as he looked out the window. Paul thought the lawman was counting every building on Main Street, like the Sheriff expected one to be missing.

"He took a hostage. There's a girl in the car with him."

Paul fought the smile that wanted to curl the corners of his lips.

The girl was Sharon Bell. Paul knew it. He'd wanted to talk to her so many times. Just to say hello. But she was always with other people. He remembered the day when she came into the store to get some parts for her daddy. She was home from college up in Greeley. The sun through the front window made her hair almost golden. Big Paul told him to get his stick and fetch two fan belts. Before she left, she looked at him for just an instant, and she said, "Thank you, Belthanger."

Now he could save her, and the whole town would see him do it.

"He's drivin' a blue Chevy coupe. If that car slows down at all, or if it acts like it's going to stop at the light, I'll tell you to take the shot."

The Sheriff took Paulie by the chin and tilted his face up. "Don't shoot if there's any chance that you might hit that girl." The sheriff took the toothpick from his mouth and flipped it out the open window. "Get ready."

Against the night sky, the stoplight blinked from green to yellow.

—

"I don't like this at all." Barker tapped the butt of a twelve-gauge shotgun on the counter. "That car should be here by now." The knuckles of his other hand turned white from his grip on the counter's edge.

Jeffery crouched behind a barrel of chains near the auto parts store's front window. He reached down and unsnapped the strap over his service revolver.

Barker told himself to breathe, and he stared down Main Street. His hand moved over the edge of the counter until his fingers touched the telephone.

—

Even in the dark, Paul knew every building and street in the town. Kingdom was too small for some. He liked it. Moonlight squeezed between the clouds and painted everything the color of an old half-dollar. The highway passed the gas station at the end of the block and swept by the sale barn at the edge of town. Farther on, the road narrowed as it crossed the fields and sagebrush pastures and turned to a gray line on the prairie.

Others his age waited to leave Kingdom. Tonight, Paul wanted to be its king.

I can do it. I'll save Sharon and kill the bank-robber.

—

The phone vibrated on the counter before Barker heard the ring. "Deputy Barker," he shouted into the mouthpiece. "Yeah, yeah—Huh?—Say that again?—I'll tell the sheriff. I'll tell him now."

He slammed the phone down and ran for the stairs. "Sheriff."

The fifth step from the top creaked under his weight. The sheriff met Barker at the top of the stairs.

"It's over, Sheriff. That bank robber's car ran out of gas and coasted to a stop three miles out of town. The Courtesy Patrol got him in handcuffs now. He never tried to fight or anything. It's over."

"What about Alice?"

"The man said she's fine. Not hurt or nothin'. It's all over, Sheriff."

The Sheriff shook out the tight ball that was his handkerchief and mopped his forehead. His chest heaved in and out. "It's over," he whispered and clamped his hand tight to the railing.

"You and Jeffery, let the town folk know they can come on out. Have 'em turn on every light in town." He nodded toward the front door. "It's over," he whispered to himself.

—

Jeffery waved his arms. The deputy pointed down Main Street. Mrs. Potter brought both hands up to her flabby face. The bank door opened, and the bank manager stepped onto the street. Under the light over the gas pumps, the man at the filling station patted the three-legged dog on the head. Kids skipped down the sidewalk like it was noon-time bright. They met their parents in front of the Rexall. Women hugged each other, and men pushed back their caps and nodded. Grandmas lifted grandbabies into their arms.

Sharon Bell held out a bottle of Dr. Pepper to Deputy Barker. He pushed her hand away, stepped closer, grabbed her by the waist, and lifted her in the air. Paul watched her hair turn into a golden fan in the yellow change of the stoplight.

—

The Sheriff unwrapped a fresh cinnamon toothpick from its wax paper and tucked it between his lips. He flipped the light switch just inside the parts store's front door and tossed his handkerchief into the wastebasket behind the counter.

Outside, Jeffery explained to Mrs. Potter and her husband how the bank robber had been captured. The man who ran The Plainsman Bar listened. Farson dropped the hood on his flatbed, poked Jeffery in the arm, and asked him to tell the story one more time.

The breeze through the open door cooled the sweat on the sheriff's face. He hitched up his gun belt, and when he stepped outside, the barmaid from the Plainsman stuck a long-neck Coors into his fist. At the intersection of Front and Main, Kingdom's only stoplight clicked from red to green.

Then, every person in Kingdom flinched at the sound.

The Sheriff wanted the crack to be thunder. But thunder didn't happen in the fall. The sound bounced off the brick storefronts and echoed down Kingdom's streets. Mrs. Potter grabbed at her chest and slumped against the Rexall's front window.

Barker shoved through the crowd of townsfolks. He pointed his pop bottle at the second-story window. "Sheriff, Belthanger just shot out the stoplight. Everybody saw him do it."

The next gunshot shook the ceiling. Something clattered onto the floor above their heads. Barker took the stairs two at a time. The fifth stair groaned under the Sheriff's bulk. Barker stopped at the door to the storeroom. He bent over, grabbed his knees and gagged. The Sheriff pushed past him. Burnt gunpowder filled the cold, stuffy air. Blood trickled from an ugly splatter on the cracked plaster wall.

"Aw, Sheriff, why would Belthanger do something like that?"

About the Author

Kevin Wolf's novel, *The Homeplace*, is the winner of the 2015 Tony Hillerman Award. The novel was a finalist for the 2016 Strand Critics Award for Debut Mystery. Western Writers of America selected his short story, "Belthanger," as the 2021 Spur Award Winner for Best Short Fiction. *Trailridge* (2024) is the first Guy Hogan Mystery. The second, *Early Snow*, will be available in November of 2025.

The great-grandson of Colorado homesteaders, he enjoys fly fishing, old Winchesters, and 1950s Western movies. He lives in Estes Park, CO, with his wife.

Visit his website: www.kevinwolfstoryteller.com